Praise for Elisa Adams *Settling the Score*

4 Blue Ribbons! "SETTLING THE SCORE is a fun, sexy read that had me hooked from the first page. I loved watching Amber's plan for revenge unfold almost as much as I loved watching them rediscover each other. Even though Jake does have his faults he is a very likable hero and you can't help but cheer for Amber. Elisa Adams has written an enjoyable read that I think everyone will enjoy." ~ *Dina Smith, Romance Junkies*

4 Stars! "I very much liked the plot premise of revenge and love...a fun and quick read..." ~ *Marcy Arbitman, Just Erotic Romance Reviews*

Settling the Score

Elisa Adams

A Samhain Publishing, Ltd. publication.

Samhain Publishing, Ltd.
2932 Ross Clark Circle, #384
Dothan, AL 36301
www.samhainpublishing.com

Settling The Score
Copyright © 2006 by Elisa Adams
Print ISBN: 1-59998-278-1
Digital ISBN: 1-59998-123-8

Editing by Sasha White
Cover by Scott Carpenter

First Samhain Publishing, Ltd. electronic publication: July 2006
First Samhain Publishing, Ltd. print publication: October 2006

Chapter One

The way Jake saw it, he had two choices. He could either pretend he didn't recognize the woman he'd just about knocked over in his rush to get to a date he didn't even want, or run like hell in the other direction. Out of the two choices, neither seemed particularly reasonable, but running held a lot of appeal.

At that moment, as he looked into familiar green eyes and caught more than a hint of humor, all the chatter in the restaurant faded to a dull roar. The music, the laughter, the clang of plates and flatware all disappeared, leaving him standing alone against the one woman he'd hoped to never see again. The only woman who'd ever been able to get under his skin and turn him inside out.

Why now? Why here, of all places? If he didn't know any better, he'd think his mother set the whole thing up, but even she wasn't that devious. He hoped.

"Hi, Jake." Amber's smooth, smoky voice rolled over him like a caress. A caress he felt everywhere. In the thirteen years since he'd last seen her, he hadn't forgotten that voice. Back in high school, it had been a voice that didn't fit her body. It fit now. *Too well.* It took him a few seconds to recover the power of speech.

"Hi."

Bumbling idiot that he'd suddenly become, he couldn't manage more than a single, lame word in response to what remained unspoken between them. All he could do was stare at the woman she'd become and wonder what had happened to the shy, overweight girl he'd known for most of his life. The one who'd hidden behind thick, plastic-framed glasses, bulky sweaters and science club meetings. Her voice was the same. Her eyes too. But everything else had changed.

He'd known about her transformation—couldn't have missed hearing about it, given that his mother and hers were best friends and two of the biggest busybodies in town—but some part of him had refused to believe it until this moment, when he'd actually gotten a chance to see what they'd been talking about. Now the woman who'd always tried her hardest to fade into the background practically screamed "notice me" without having to say a word. He'd noticed. Taken inventory of every inch of her.

"How have you been?" she continued, humor glinting in those big green eyes. She smelled like flowers and some sort of exotic spice. It hit him like a punch in the gut and stirred parts of his body he tried to will to remain dormant. The last thing he needed right now was a hard-on. She'd slap him for sure.

"Jake?" Her husky laugh alerted him to the fact he had yet to answer her question.

"I...uh...I'm good." *Good? Freakin' stupid response, moron. Anything else you'd like to do to make a fool of yourself?* All those years at Harvard, and he was reduced to an incoherent idiot when faced with a beautiful woman.

No. Not just any beautiful woman. He'd dated his fair share of them, and none had ever affected him the way Amber was tonight. There was something about her that made his brain threaten to shut down. He cleared his throat. "How have you been?"

"I've been great. It's good to see you."

It was more than good to see her. The second their bodies had touched, every single one of his nerves had stood up and taken notice. Yet another hazard of running smack-dab into a beautiful, curvy woman.

She *was* beautiful, too. In a way he never would have imagined. All lean lines and gentle curves. Even her hair had changed. What used to be a long, frizzy mess had turned into shiny curls the color of black coffee. Her natural color, he knew, and it complemented the rich, warm tones of her caramel skin. The curls fell to just below her shoulders and made him want to tangle his fingers in them to see if they were really as soft as they looked.

Her dress was red. Short and tight enough to afford him a good look at her nipped waist above slightly flared hips. Cut low enough it revealed a mouth-watering amount of cleavage. She had to be wearing heels—four-inchers, since the top of her head was at his eye level. *Shit.* He loved a woman in heels. The higher the better. Maybe it was a little shallow, but he'd always been a visual kind of guy.

Spiked heels and a red dress. Guaranteed to make him go rock-solid in seconds flat. He swallowed hard. Here he was, meeting another woman for a blind date he'd rather avoid, and all he could think about was a woman who wouldn't want *him*.

"You look good, Amber." The words slipped out before he could pull them back, and he muttered a curse. He would not, *would not*, hit on Amber Velez, no matter how much his body begged. She wouldn't be interested, and even if she was, he didn't deserve a second chance. She'd trusted him once, a long time ago, and he'd trampled on her feelings. She wasn't the kind of woman to forgive a betrayal like that so easily.

Her gaze left his and traveled down his body in a slow perusal that had him clenching his hands into fists. For a woman who shouldn't be interested, she certainly didn't act the part. By the time her gaze came back to his, he couldn't stand still.

"You look good, too, Jake. Amazing, actually. Though I have to say, I'm not surprised."

He glanced at her, trying to read her expression. She didn't mean the compliment. Couldn't. Not after what had happened between them.

And that was the reason he had to walk away. No sense hoping for something that wouldn't happen in this lifetime. "It's good to see you, too. Really good. I'm sorry, but I have to go. I'm meeting someone here and I don't want to be late. This blind date thing my mother set up. I'll talk to you later, okay?"

He stepped around her, further into the dark-paneled waiting area at the front of the restaurant, and started for the podium where the hostess stood. A quick glance at his watch told him it was just after seven. With any luck, this date wouldn't be like the last one and freak out that he showed up thirty seconds past the agreed-upon meeting time. The last woman his mother set him up with had been a little…off-center, so it had taken over six months and a lot of persuading to get him to agree to meet up with her latest pick.

He stopped at the podium and gave his name to the young, red-headed hostess. "Jake Storm. I'm meeting someone here. We have reservations for seven o'clock."

"Your date is already here." The hostess glanced over his shoulder before her gaze returned to his. She wrinkled her nose. "You were just talking to her a second ago."

It took a little while for her words to register. When they did, he shook his head. His stomach bottomed out and his hands clenched into involuntary fists. *No way.* No freakin' way would his mother do that to him.

He ran through what she'd told him in his head. Short and slim with curly dark hair and green eyes and…

Shit. A muscle in his jaw ticked. Now his mother had crossed the line. Setting him up with an ex-girlfriend? What had made her think that was a good idea?

There was only one explanation. She'd finally gone over the deep end. The woman was a mental case, and despite the fact he was grateful to her for giving birth to him, he wasn't about to let her get away with this crap anymore. She needed to be set straight. No more blind dates for him. Ever. He had enough irritation and discomfort at work. He didn't need it trickling over into his social life.

His brothers Brian and David were still single. Their mother could set her sights on them, because Jake had had enough.

"Jake? Are you okay?" Amber's voice dragged him back to the present.

He relaxed his hands and shook his head to clear the aggravation. Now Amber would really hate him. As if she hadn't had ample reason before tonight. He turned around, his arms outstretched and his palms up in a gesture of surrender. "I'm sorry. I didn't realize my mother was going to do this. If I had, I would have put a stop to it before this whole mess even got started."

Amber didn't even hesitate. "I'm glad she didn't tell you."

The humor in her eyes made his own narrow. Why did she not look as shocked by the turn of events as he felt? "What's going on?"

She knew. Had probably known the whole time, and she hadn't bothered to say a word. He shoved his hands into the pockets of his pants and let out a breath. This couldn't be happening. *No way.* This was the exact reason he couldn't stand blind dates. They never turned out the way a person expected and ended up being more trouble than they were worth. Especially when one of the participants had an advantage, like knowing the "blind date" setup was a lie.

Amber walked closer and put her hand on his arm. The heat of her palm scorched him through his dress shirt, damn it, and it made him grit his teeth. His mother had managed to pull one over on him and she'd dragged Amber into it this time. Why the hell did it have to be Amber? Any other woman would have been a better choice.

"Don't be mad at your mother," Amber whispered. She smiled up at him.

Jake shivered. It was like she was reading his mind. Being the same age, Jake and Amber had spent a lot of time together as kids. She'd been able to read his thoughts back then. It shocked him that she was still able to do it, even after all the years they'd been apart. It was a comforting feeling, but the anxiety far outweighed the comfort. "Why shouldn't I be mad at her? She's taken this quest for marrying me off too far this time. It's one thing to set me up with a complete stranger, but this is different. She never should have dragged you into it."

The look in Amber's eyes told him she was about to say something he wouldn't like. She didn't disappoint. "This was my idea. I asked her to do it."

His face heated. He took a step back, dislodging her hand. "What? Why would you do that? I don't like being tricked."

"I didn't think you'd want to see me if I just called."

Damned right he wouldn't have. It wasn't because of her, though. His guilt would have driven him to turn down her request. Amber hadn't done anything wrong. The blame for the incident that had caused the rift between them rested solely on his shoulders.

He ran a hand through his hair, trying to calm his raging emotions. Part of him wanted to storm out of the restaurant without looking back, but another part wouldn't let him. He was curious to hear what she had to say.

"Sir? Your table is ready if you'd both like to follow me."

He glanced at the hostess, who stood in the doorway to the main dining room, holding a couple of leather-bound menus. Her eyebrows were raised and she kept looking back and forth between Amber and him.

Dinner was out of the question. If Amber wanted to talk to him, she'd have to settle for doing it somewhere else. "Thanks, but I think we're going to have to—"

"Thank you," Amber interrupted. "Lead the way."

She grabbed Jake's hand and pulled him after the hostess, following her toward a small, semi-private table in the back of the crowded dining room. Still in shock at the way Amber had taken charge without even asking him what he wanted to do, Jake wasn't able to say anything until the hostess set the menus on the table and walked away.

Once they were alone, Amber settled into a chair and glanced up at Jake, tapping cherry-red fingernails on the wooden tabletop. Uncertainty tinged her gaze, but it didn't replace the damned amusement. "Aren't you going to sit down?"

"I haven't decided yet."

If he sat, he'd have to talk to her. If they talked, she'd want to rehash a past he'd just as soon forget. Women were like that. Always wanting to *talk* about every little thing. Over and over. Usually until he felt like his head would burst. If he had to listen to hours of Amber berating him for the jerk he'd been... Well, he could think of about a thousand other things he'd rather be doing. Like walking across hot coals, naked, with a swarm of hornets chasing him. He knew how much of a jerk he'd been. Had berated himself enough over the years for ruining the best friendship he'd ever had. He didn't need her to rub it in any further.

In typical Amber fashion, she rolled her eyes. "If this is about what happened in the past, don't worry about it. I was over that a month after it happened."

"Really?" He searched her face for clues to her true motive. In his experience, women rarely said what they meant. They'd tell a man one thing, let him get comfortable with it, and then say something totally contradictory. He'd given up trying to understand women years ago and had only been happier since.

"Yeah, really." She wrinkled her nose. "We were kids then. Eighteen years old is hardly worldly. Teenagers make mistakes. It's part of life. I don't know about you, but I've grown up since then. Sit down, Jake."

He didn't miss the little dig she'd made and it prodded him to flop into the seat across from her, though he wasn't about to pretend to like it. Amber and his mother had conned him into this, but it didn't mean he had to force himself to have a good time.

"Was that so difficult?"

He narrowed his eyes. It was freakin' hell. Of course it would be easier for her. She'd known all along. She'd had time to prepare, while he'd been left floundering around like a fish out of water.

They sat in silence for a little while, Amber's attention elsewhere and Jake not knowing what to say to keep up the conversation. She glanced at her menu and it gave him the chance to search her expression. The humor was still there, front and center. She was toying with him. Jerking him around like a cat chasing a mouse. That small bit of information should have irritated him, but it didn't. It intrigued him instead.

He sat back in the wooden chair and smiled. Amber had always been quiet and unassuming before. Not anymore. She had spunk now. He liked that. A lot. He couldn't tear his gaze away from her. It wasn't her looks, though they were definitely a big draw, but it was something else. The spark of life in her eyes attracted him on so many levels. It also told him she wasn't an easy woman to handle.

Good. He'd always loved a challenge.

Most of his discomfort with the situation faded to the background. If she was over the past, he could get over it, too. She'd set this little farce of a blind date up, dressed in a way that told him she wanted him to notice. He had. Immediately. He wanted his hands all over her. No doubt his primal reaction had been her intention. Now he had to figure out why she'd gone to all the trouble. If she'd just wanted to talk, as she'd told him, she could have come to his office.

She didn't look like a woman who wanted to do much talking.

A small smile curved her lips, but she didn't glance up from the menu. "Do you know what you want to eat?"

Yeah, he knew. It had nothing to do with food. His appetite for anything culinary had faded the second his body had smacked into hers. "I guess."

He picked up the menu and started thumbing through it, not really seeing the words printed on the page. This promised to be an interesting evening, and he couldn't wait to see how things played out. She'd reveal what she wanted soon, and with any luck, it would be the same thing he wanted.

"Your mother tells me you're a lawyer now," Amber said after the waitress had come to take their orders.

"Yeah. I have an office downtown."

"I know," she told him with a wink. "In the building your parents own."

Had she been snooping? He leaned forward. "How did you know that?"

"Your mother told me. She thought I might like to know who my new neighbors will be."

Was she saying what he thought she was saying? He let out a breath. Of course she was. Of-freakin'-course. Typical woman, dropping something so huge on him like she'd just told him the sky was cloudy tonight. "You're going to be renting that tiny little third-floor apartment?"

She nodded. "I sure am. And the second floor office, too."

"For what?" He picked up his water glass and swirled the ice cubes around for a few seconds before taking a sip. This ought to be good.

All through school, she'd talked about becoming a doctor. Was that what she was doing here? Opening a medical practice?

He shook his head. In that dress and those heels, she didn't look like any doctor he'd ever known.

"I'm renting the office for my business. I'm a wedding planner."

He coughed and sputtered. The water he'd been sipping caught in his throat. The glass hit the table with a thump and a swish of water. Several other diners glanced their way, their gazes a good mix of aggravation, concern and amusement.

It took Jake a few seconds to be able to breathe right again, and even then he had trouble quieting the cough caused by water going down the wrong pipe. She had to be kidding. "A *wedding* planner? Like white dresses and walks down the aisle and shit? Are you serious?"

She nodded, her expression solemn, but that same damned glint of humor danced in her eyes. Forearms on the table, he leaned toward her. *A wedding planner.* He never would have figured. And she was renting the office directly above his. A recipe for disaster if he'd ever seen one. "My mother did tell you that I'm a *divorce* lawyer, right?"

"She might have mentioned that." A smile played at the corners of her lips. She ran her fingertip along the rim of her water glass. When she spoke again, her voice was barely above a whisper. "You don't look happy, Jake. Is this going to be a problem for you? I hope not, because I really have my heart set on that office. The layout is perfect for what I need."

He let out a breath. He was being a first-class jerk, but really, had she been expecting anything different? He'd spent the better portion of his teenage years treating her like crap. The only difference was she'd let him get away with it back then. He had a feeling the woman she'd become wouldn't be as forgiving.

"Why would it be a problem?" It wouldn't be *a* problem. It would be a whole host of them, one right after another. Amber renting the office above his was asking for trouble. Just freakin' great. A wedding planner upstairs from a divorce lawyer. Talk about one-stop shopping. At least he'd get some free advertising out of the deal. When her clients' marriages dissolved, they'd know where to go to fix the issues. "Of course it's no problem. What made you get into that field, anyway?"

In school she'd been so ambitious, if not a little shy. He'd always thought, if she could get over the shyness, she could take over the damned world. Why wedding planning, of all things? He didn't know much about the career as a whole, but it didn't seem like it would take a higher education to help someone pick out flowers and a caterer.

"During college I majored in business and took a job as a secretary at the office of a wedding planner to pay for school, and everything just snowballed from there. My boss retired a few weeks ago, so I decided to move back home and start my own business."

"Does it make you happy?" he asked before he could pull the words back. "You know, planning other people's weddings?"

"If it didn't make me happy, I wouldn't bother doing it." She lifted the glass to her lips and took a delicate sip of water.

The way her fingers curled around the thin, tall glass made him think of them curled around the part of his anatomy currently vying for her attention. He tried to shake off the ever-increasing arousal, but there was no pushing it aside. Amber had grown into a fascinating woman and he wanted to get the chance to know her better. A lot better. But not sitting in a crowded restaurant. What he had in mind required some serious one-on-one time.

He muttered a curse. If she knew the direction his thoughts kept taking, she'd kick his shin with the pointed toe of her shoe. Here she was, trying to have a serious conversation with him, and he couldn't get past the fact that her legs would feel amazing wrapped around his waist. He swallowed hard and forced himself to listen.

"I spent so much of my high-school career worrying about doing well in school, getting into a good college and getting a great job, that I didn't leave time to think about what was important," she continued with a shrug. "My parents wanted me to be a doctor. It took me a while to realize it wasn't what *I* wanted. Finally, I'd just had enough and I decided to do things my own way. My own way turned out to be a lot different than anyone expected, even me. I get a lot of satisfaction out of helping women plan the weddings of their dreams. Plus, you know me with organization. My mother says I should have minored in it in college. This really is the perfect job for me."

Had to be a woman thing. He'd never really understood why they went nuts over—and spent tens of thousands of dollars on—something that would last a few hours. He'd seen his mother in a frenzy planning his sister Amanda's weddings, all four of them, and had shaken his head at the whole ordeal every time. He'd seen it all. The chaos. The tears. The mood swings that made any sane man in the area want to run and hide.

And forget the groom. He was lucky if he even got to choose what color tux he wore, let alone make decisions regarding the ceremony or the reception. The way Jake saw it, it had to be some kind of temporary insanity that compelled normally sane women to act like total nutcases whenever someone so much as mentioned the words "I do".

Then again, maybe he was a little too biased to judge. In his line of work, he saw what happened after the honeymoon ended and couples realized they weren't as perfect for each other as they'd first thought. The backstabbing. The fighting. Custody battles—even over dogs and cats and one time over a car. The whole marriage thing was a big waste of time. Fifty percent of marriages ended in divorce, anyway, so what was the point in even going there in the first place?

"What's the matter?" Amber asked. "You're starting to look a little shell-shocked."

"Nah. Just surprised. I'm glad you're happy, though."

She smiled. "Thanks."

They lapsed into silence for a little while, with only the occasional conversation, until the waitress brought their meals. Steak for him and a salad for Amber. It gave him a small measure of relief to see that the salad was huge—and had chicken on top. He preferred women to actually eat when he took them out, rather than graze on rabbit food.

"I didn't lose all the weight by eating cheeseburgers," she told him, her tone laced with laughter. "I'm not one of those women who can eat whatever she wants. I've learned to take care of myself."

"I didn't say a word."

"You didn't need to." She reached out and brushed her fingertips over the top of his hand, sending a shock of heat up his arm. "You have very expressive eyes. I've always liked that about you. I'm glad that hasn't changed."

He dropped his gaze to the table and focused on the plate of food in front of him. No one but Amber had ever told him that. As far as he knew, no one else had even noticed. It unnerved him that she could see right through him, no matter how she did it.

Slowly, he started to relax again and by the time they were halfway through their meals, they were deep in conversation. Amber told Jake about her life in a New York suburb, and he filled her in on his family and some of the things that had been going on in Lilton in the years she'd been away.

A familiar voice from a nearby table drew his attention. He glanced at the tall, thin blonde and his breath stuck in his throat. Madison. *Shit.* Like he needed this right now.

He tried to focus on his conversation with Amber, but his gaze kept straying back to the table a few away from theirs, where Madison sat with an older, gray-haired man. Every once in a while, she touched the man's arm and seemed to be laughing at almost everything he said. Jake narrowed his eyes. Was nothing sacred anymore? What gave her the right to parade around town with someone else?

"What's wrong?"

He snapped his gaze back to Amber's and shook his head. "It's nothing."

"An old girlfriend?"

Not hardly. He let out a bitter laugh. "You remember Steve Caldwell?"

She nodded. "Big blond guy. Football player."

"Yeah. That woman is Madison. His wife. Well, for a little while longer, at least. They're getting a divorce."

"You don't look happy about it."

Why should he? Two of his best friends were splitting up and they wanted him to choose sides. How the hell was he supposed to do that? Steve had been his friend longer, but over the past seven years, he'd gotten close to Madison, too. They were both like family, and neither of them seemed to understand that he didn't want to be in the middle of the mess they'd created—another reason why he didn't believe in marriage. The people getting the divorce were never the only ones hurt.

"It's a bad situation. I can't stand to see two people I'm close to in the middle of this crap."

Her eyebrows shot up. "You're not involved? I mean, you aren't representing either of them?"

Hell, no. He'd been against the whole thing since Steve had confessed to him a few months ago that he'd asked Madison for a divorce. Tried to talk him out of it, even, but Steve had been insistent. They'd married too young. Hadn't really taken the time to get to know each other first. The passion had faded from their marriage. Jake had heard all the excuses, but he had a feeling Steve had left out one important detail. The truth. "No. I told them both to find other lawyers. It would be a conflict of interest."

Amber's hand came down on his and she squeezed. "For what it's worth, I'm sorry."

"Yeah, me too." He wanted to pull his hand back, but he didn't. It felt good to have her touching him. "I'm having a good time. I don't want anything to ruin that. I'm sorry. Forget any of that happened, okay?"

"Are you? Having a good time, I mean. I know I should have been honest with you. I'm sorry I tricked you into this. I don't want you mad at me."

"Yeah. I'm having a good time. I should be upset, but I'm not. It's been fun." She was still fun to be with, even though now she was so much bolder than she used to be. He could see himself spending a lot more time with her.

"It has. I didn't think it would go this smoothly." She smiled, and this time he didn't feel like she was taunting him. It was a genuine smile that warmed him from the inside out. All the old feelings he'd had for her resurfaced and he nearly choked on them. Their relationship had been complicated in the past, but he had a feeling it had nothing on what was about to happen to them now.

If she was telling him the truth.

He frowned. Where had that thought come from? She'd said she wanted to see him. Why couldn't he take her words at face value?

Because he knew women enough to know they rarely meant what they said, and it took them forever to get over grudges. He wanted to spend more time with Amber, but at the same time, he had to tread carefully. He could enjoy spending time with her without getting attached.

"Attached" was something he didn't do. Ever. Years ago, he'd decided against long-term commitment. Maybe it had been seeing his sister go through three divorces. Maybe it had been the way his mother had started pushing for grandkids the day he graduated college. Whatever it was, he'd sworn a while back that he'd never settle down with any one woman. Amber would be no exception, but he had a feeling she didn't want anything more from him than he wanted from her. That thought eased his mind and he was able to enjoy the rest of dinner.

By the time they finished the meal and headed out to the parking lot, Jake knew he had to see her again. It didn't matter what she and his mother had done. Didn't matter what her ulterior motives were. The spark that had always been between them hadn't gone away. It seemed even stronger now than ever. He couldn't walk away from her this time, and he couldn't let her walk away, either. Not without seeing where whatever was happening between them might go.

The thought should have scared him. Over the past few years, working with one divorcing couple after another, he'd learned that marriage wasn't for him. His mother wouldn't accept it. Half the women he dated didn't believe it. But it was the truth. He was a bachelor for life, and a woman like Amber threatened his sense of security. He could tell himself over and over that he wouldn't get involved any deeper than a casual fling, but what good did that do him when the woman was the whole package? Beauty, brains and a sense of humor. He should be running away as fast as he could, but instead he found himself following her into the parking lot like some lovesick puppy dog craving a tiny second of her attention.

Friggin' sick, Jake. Totally twisted. Like he needed this crap in his life.

He shook off the conflicting emotions and turned his attention back to Amber. "Where did you park?"

"This way." Without waiting for him, she took off to the right. He started to follow, but stopped when he got a good look at her ass under the tight fabric of the dress. It was rounded and full, and perfect enough to make his mouth water. *Everything* about her made his mouth water, and that fact only increased his confusion over the whole situation. He needed to get his head on straight before he said or did something stupid.

One minute she'd aroused his mind, the next his body. One second he wanted to turn around and walk away from her, and in the next he wanted to pull her closer. The whole thing was crazy. Absolutely nuts, and he should be steering clear of her. But he couldn't. Not yet, anyway. For some reason, not getting a chance to see her again made his stomach ache.

The thought of seeing more of her made other parts of his body ache. He shifted and briefly considered untucking his shirt to disguise the bulge of his burgeoning erection, but it wouldn't matter. There was no way to hide it. In just a few hours, she'd managed to tie him in knots.

Amber turned around and laughed. "You okay?"

No. Definitely not okay. Since he couldn't think of a single thing to say that didn't include "bedroom" and "now", he just nodded and followed her toward her car.

He wouldn't touch her tonight, no matter how much he wanted to. By some strange twist of fate she'd decided he deserved a second chance, and he wouldn't ruin it by acting like a teenager. They were adults now. Adults dated at least a few times before they jumped into bed. After what had happened in the past, she already thought he had no restraint. Now was his chance to prove otherwise. No, he wouldn't touch her tonight, but after that all bets were off. He *would* convince her to go out with him again. On his terms. He fully intended to take some time getting to know her a lot better.

She stopped next to a vintage black sports car a few rows over from where he'd parked. "This is me."

"Nice car." Yet another surprise. He'd pictured her in something newer. Sensible and safe. "It must have a lot of power."

"You have no idea." She winked. "I like power."

The look she gave him had him squirming where he stood. "Oh, yeah?"

"Uh-huh."

She unlocked the doors with the small remote attached to her key ring, and before she could open the door, he stepped around her and did it for her.

Amber laughed. "What are you doing?"

Though she might not have noticed due to his uncharacteristic behavior at dinner, he'd been raised to be a gentleman. His parents had made sure he knew how to treat a woman. Tonight, Amber had set him off balance with her blind-date scheme, and it had taken him until right about now to recover.

"I didn't pull out your chair at the restaurant, and you wouldn't let me hold the door for you when we were leaving."

She raised her eyebrows. For a few seconds, he thought she might laugh at him, but in the end she simply shook her head. "I don't need that kind of stuff, Jake. Chivalry is unnecessary as far as I'm concerned. I'm a take-charge kind of girl now, in case you hadn't noticed."

He gritted his teeth. He'd noticed. Noticed and damned near drooled over it, among other things, but his upbringing wouldn't let him ignore the basic principles he'd been raised with. "My mother raised me to be polite."

"She raised you well. I won't deny it. But you don't have to cater to me. I can take care of myself. I've been doing that for a long time now, and I turned out just fine. If I want something, I know how to get it, and I don't stop until I do."

In the next second, much to his surprise, she wrapped her fingers around his neck and pulled him down for a kiss.

Chapter Two

Amber sank into the kiss, reveling in the feel of Jake so close to her. He stiffened at first, probably due to surprise, but within seconds he managed to take over the kiss in a big way. The warm, spicy taste of him in her mouth as he stroked his tongue inside made her shiver right to her toes. The man could still kiss. He hadn't lost that ability. If anything, he had gotten better with time.

She tangled the fingers of her free hand in the front of his shirt and drew him even closer, suddenly needing to feel Jake's hard body pressed right up against hers. Lord knew the man *should* be a great kisser. He'd had a lot of practice.

She'd been away from town since college, with only the occasional weekend visit back home to see her family, but stories of Jake's exploits had still reached her via her younger sister. Adele, the gossip-queen-in-training, had relished telling her about his latest conquest. Amber had never had the guts to tell her sister how much it killed her to hear the stories. She'd never told *anyone* what had happened between her and Jake, for good reason.

Amber herself had held the title of Stupid Woman Who'd Believed Jake Storm's Lies before, and she refused to hold it again. She was a lot stronger now than she'd been that summer after high school, and a lot less infatuated, too. She was in complete control. If anything happened between them now, tonight or later, it would be on her terms. *If* they slept together, he would be the one who was the conquest this time.

The man deserved to be knocked down a few pegs, and she was just the woman to do it. He needed to learn that this was the twenty-first century. It wasn't okay to treat women like doormats anymore. Women weren't disposable, no matter what some men thought.

Zack had never treated her like a disposable woman, but then again Zack had never turned her on the way Jake could with just a look. And his kiss...if they hadn't been in the middle of a public parking lot, she had a feeling she'd have already torn off his clothes.

His hands landed on her hips and she knew it was time to break the kiss. Couldn't let him get carried away. If he did, she might too, and then she'd really be in trouble. Just because almost every other single woman in town jumped right into his bed didn't mean she would. At least not again. The first time, she'd been young and stupid and in love. Now that had all changed. She wasn't young or stupid anymore, and love really had no place in her life right now. There were too many things she wanted to do first. Years ago, she'd gone to sleep every night wishing he'd propose after high-school graduation. Now she was glad he hadn't. She hadn't known who she was then, but she knew now. The woman she'd become had no interest in long-term commitment.

She stepped away and brushed her finger down his cheek, taking in the sight of him for about the hundredth time that evening. He'd outgrown that lanky, baseball-player look he'd had back in high school and had grown into his broad shoulders. Though his features were essentially the same, they'd matured. His blue eyes hadn't changed, and the small wrinkles around them let her know he still laughed and smiled as much as he used to. His hair was still dark, though the short, spiky cut was a change from the shaggy style he used to wear.

All in all, Jake Storm was an incredible package. Time had increased his sex appeal rather than diminished it. She needed to call it a night before she forgot all her plans and did something stupid, like invite him back to her apartment.

"It's getting late. I need to get home now. I'll talk to you later, okay?"

His shoulders heaved and he looked like he might protest for a second, but then he backed up a step and shook his head, his gaze uncertain. "Does that mean you don't want me to call you?"

She should have said no. Should have made him wait, but something inside her wouldn't let her. He wanted to call. That meant she'd hooked him already. A smile tickled the corners of her lips. "No, it doesn't. I'd like you to call…if you're really going to do it this time."

"I'll call. I promise."

The same guilt she'd seen often during the meal flashed across his gaze and it weakened her resolve to teach him a lesson. Maybe he really had changed.

Didn't matter. According to Adele, and Jake's sister Rachel, he hadn't changed that much. He dated a different woman every Friday night and dumped them by Sunday morning. "Okay. Let me see your cell phone. I'll program my number in."

He unhooked the phone from the clip on his belt and handed it to her. She programmed the number in and gave the phone back.

"Thanks." The smile he shot her was anything but casual, and her panties dampened. Part of her wanted to invite him home with her tonight, but she held the words back. No way in hell could she be that weak. It was just residual attraction from years ago. That was all. Once she spent more time with him, she'd get over it. He'd prove to her what a chauvinistic cad he really was, and then she'd be left wondering yet again what she'd ever seen in him.

He clipped the phone back on his belt and cupped her cheek in his palm for a brief second. All too soon, he let go and dropped his arm to his side. "I'll call you tomorrow."

Yeah, right. "So soon?"

"Yeah."

The single word spoken in his deep, smooth voice coupled with the look in his eyes sent a shiver through her. She wasn't the only one affected by the impromptu kiss. It shook him as much as it shook her, and the thought made her smile inside. *Step one, accomplished.* He was interested. Unfortunately, so was she, as much as she tried to deny it.

And if she didn't get out of there soon, she ran the risk of spoiling everything she'd been planning since deciding to move back to town. There were things to be accomplished. Things that didn't involve falling in love with Jake Storm all over again. "Great. I'll talk to you then."

Without another word, she climbed into her car, started it up, and pulled out of the parking space. A quick glance in her rearview mirror let her know he stood there, watching her, as she left the parking lot and headed for home.

It wasn't until she'd driven into the parking lot in back of her building that the reality of the situation hit her. The man was still as potent as ever, and if she wasn't careful, she'd end up in way too deep.

ରେ ରେ ରେ

"Would you mind explaining to me what the heck you were thinking?"

Jake's mother glanced up from the stove and blinked at him, her expression suspiciously innocent. "I don't know what you're talking about."

The sunlight filling the bright, yellow and white kitchen made him want to shield his eyes. The unmistakable scents of morning filled the room. Bacon, sausage, pancakes and syrup. His stomach turned over. Eight a.m. wasn't usually too early for him, but sleep had been hard to come by last night, leaving him exhausted. Trying to get her to confess the truth—the real truth—promised to be a battle he didn't need. He would have skipped out on the traditional family breakfast had he not wanted to grill his mother about her motives for agreeing to Amber's ridiculous plan. Her answers wouldn't come easily. The wide-eyed innocent act told him that much.

He shook his head. He didn't even know where to begin. "The whole purpose of a blind date is going out with someone you *don't* know. A complete stranger. Setting me up with a…a friend kind of defeats the purpose."

His mother stirred the scrambled eggs in the cast-iron skillet with a wooden spoon. "Would you rather I find someone you haven't met before for next time? I can do that, if you'd rather."

"No." *Hell, no.* His days of being coerced into blind dates were officially over. It was well past time to put his foot down. "No more set-ups, strangers or otherwise. Last night could have been a huge, uncomfortable mess. You should have known that going into it."

She only smiled. "Are you saying you didn't have a good time? I'm surprised. You and Amber always got along well before."

She had no idea how well they'd gotten along. Better than anyone around them had ever known. "No, I'm not saying that. It was…interesting catching up with an old friend. I just don't like surprises, and that was one hell of a surprise the two of you threw at me."

"Watch your language. And why do you have such a hard time admitting you had fun? Amber is a wonderful girl, and she's so pretty now." She set the spoon on the counter and propped her hands on her hips. "Don't think I don't know what went on between you two. I know you were more than friends, so you can cut that act right now, young man."

"Excuse me?" He rolled his head from side to side and swallowed down a yawn. After a sleepless night, tossing and turning, wishing Amber had been there in bed with him, he was in no shape to deal with anything so early in the morning, let alone this.

"I know exactly how close the two of you were. Do you think I didn't notice that you spent all your free time with her, and then suddenly stopped talking to her? I swear, Jacob, walking away from that woman was probably one of the stupidest things you've ever done. Look what it's done to you."

He let out a breath. He had no patience for woman riddles this early in the morning. "What are you talking about? It hasn't done anything to me."

"You just keep telling yourself that." She went back to cooking the usual huge Storm family breakfast, ignoring him for all of two seconds before she spoke again. "Don't you see it? She's the reason you can't commit to any other woman. You compare all of them to Amber. You know, in your heart, that she's the right woman for you. No wonder why you get bored with your girlfriends so quickly."

He scrubbed a hand down his face. Of all the random, off-the-wall assumptions to make. He loved his mother, but the woman was insane. "I'm not interested in a commitment with anyone. It has nothing to do with Amber. Until last night, I hadn't even seen her in thirteen years, and I hadn't thought about her in just as long. Believe me, she has no bearing on my decision. I like my life the way it is, and I'm not willing to start compromising on the way I want to do things. How can you even jump to that kind of a conclusion?"

"A mother knows these things." She gave him a small wink. "That's just the way it is. Have some coffee, dear. You look like you could use it."

He needed something a lot stronger than coffee at the moment, but he'd settle for what he could get. He walked over to the cabinet, grabbed a blue stoneware mug, and filled it with fresh, hot coffee from the carafe. He added a healthy splash of cream and took a sip. About seven more cups of the stuff and he'd be back to normal.

"You still didn't answer my question. What were you thinking? Amber said it was her idea, and after talking to her last night I'm sure it was, but why would you go along with it without giving me some kind of warning?"

"Because she asked me not to tell you." She shot him a look that said "duh" better than words ever could. "Amber asked me to keep it a secret. She just wanted to talk to you, Jake. What's the harm in that?"

Things could get out of control more quickly than he could handle if he wasn't careful. Amber wasn't like the women he usually dated. She had the potential to put a wrench in the life he'd spent so much time building for himself. Plus there was the guilt that still nagged him. He didn't think he'd ever be able to completely get rid of that.

"I'm your son. Aren't you supposed to be on my side in this?"

She turned the stove burner off, scooped the cooked eggs into a serving bowl, and set it on the counter next to plates filled with bacon, pancakes and toast. "I am on your side. Of course I am. Why would you think different?"

Ha! Since when was she on his side? He took another sip of coffee before setting the mug on the counter and rolling his shoulders in frustration. "No, you aren't. If you were on my side, you would have told me what Amber had planned. But you didn't. You didn't say a word. You ambushed me last night. Both of you did. That isn't right."

"It's very right. Probably the most right thing that's happened to you in a long time. You'll see that someday soon." His mother picked up a plate of pancakes and thrust it in his direction. "While you're in here with me instead of watching the news with your father and brothers, you might want to make yourself useful and help me bring all the food out to the table. And make sure you eat a big breakfast today. You're going to need the energy later."

He took the plate from her hands, trying to stomp down the sliver of dread that speared his gut at her words and her devious expression. Now what was she up to? "What did you do, Mom?"

"Nothing." She shook her head and pasted on that wide-eyed innocent expression again. He nearly snorted. "Amber and Adele are painting the office starting today. It's just the two of them, and there's a lot of wall space to paint, so if they work alone it's going to take them all week. It would be nice to go and offer them a little help, don't you think?"

"No. No way. If Amber needed help, she would have asked. You're not going to get in the middle of this, Mom. I don't need to be fixed up. I have no problem finding dates on my own."

"You're thirty-one. Are you engaged yet?"

"No." *Thank God.*

"Then it seems to me you do have a problem. You need to settle down. You're not getting any younger. By now, you should already have a wife and a couple of kids."

He fought a groan. Just the thought of being responsible for a wife—and children—made his stomach hurt. "I'm not interested in getting married. Ever."

"That's because you had the right woman once, and you let her go." She patted his arm before picking up the bowl of eggs. "Don't worry. I'll help you. I won't let you let her get away this time."

Without waiting for a response, she walked out of the room, leaving him alone and thinking he should duck out before the situation got any worse.

No. It was too late for that. The second Amber had been to see his mother with her blind-date scheme, the damage had been done. Now he just hoped he could do a little damage control before things got out of hand.

He followed her out of the kitchen, already brainstorming a plan in his mind. Marriage wasn't for him, no matter how much his mother might push for it. Besides, he had a feeling Amber hadn't been entirely truthful about her intentions. She had other things in mind besides resolving the issues they'd had in the past.

He shook his head. What an absolute mess this had turned into. Something told him that, between his mother and Amber, it could only get worse from here. It was an explosion waiting to happen, and all he could do was wait and watch. He just hoped he'd be able to extricate himself from the volatile situation before the two women brought him down with them.

ରେ ରେ ରେ

"How did your date go last night?"

Amber squinted through the bright sunlight streaming through the still-curtainless windows in the office at her sister's cheerful expression. Adele stood in front of her, wet paintbrush in one hand and the other hand propped on her denim-clad hip. Her sneakered foot tapped on the dusty floor.

"Did you hear me?" she asked, a giggle in her tone. She ran a hand through her short black hair. "Earth to Amber. It must have been one hell of a date for you to be so out of it the next day."

Amber shook her head. *Give me a break.* She barely resisted the urge to wrap her fingers around her sister's throat and squeeze until all the cheerfulness dropped from her expression. As far as Amber was concerned, no one should have the right to so much as smile before nine in the morning.

"I'm not *out of it* because of the date. I'm out of it because you dragged me out of bed practically before the sun even came up and forced me to come down here and *work*. All before my coffee has even kicked in to boot. You know I'm not a morning person."

Amber narrowed her eyes at Adele's smile. How could anyone be this happy at eight in the morning? Amber had yet to even wake up, though she'd been out of bed for a little over an hour. The paint fumes permeating the air should have helped, but so far, they'd only given her a headache.

Amber hadn't rolled out of bed at the crack of dawn like Adele, but had at least managed to get up at the closest time physically possible for her. Seven a.m. was too early, but Adele had called and said she was on her way over with coffee, and that Amber needed to get her lazy butt out of bed so they could work on getting the office ready to open.

Adele was right, of course. Things needed to get done, but Amber would prefer to do her painting in the evening, when she could actually keep her eyes open.

"I know, but you aren't usually this grumpy." Adele wrinkled her nose. Amusement sparkled in her hazel eyes. "So I figure whoever you went out with must have kept you up pretty late and worn you out. Will you tell me how it went already? You seem to forget, I've been married to the same man for eight years. I love Max, but I miss the thrill of a new date every once in a while, so I have to live vicariously through you, my very single sister."

Adele's good humor was infectious, and Amber had to laugh. "Okay. It went fine. Why are you so anxious to hear about it?"

"You seem...spacey today. It must have been an interesting evening."

"You don't even know the half of it."

"So why don't you tell me?"

Some things were better left unsaid. She had yet to explain to Adele that she was seeing Jake again, even if she did have ulterior motives this time. She had no need of a lecture from her happily-married-with-children sister. Adele had given her a lecture the first time she'd started seeing Jake, though back then he'd wanted to keep it a secret. Adele, the mother hen, had been worried about Amber and she'd been very vocal in her concerns. Amber didn't need the concern now, not like she had then. If she mentioned Jake, it would bring about a whole bunch of questions she didn't have answers to.

"You don't need to know. I'd like to keep my private life private, if you don't mind."

She realized Adele was staring past her toward the door and Amber spun around, sloshing lukewarm coffee over the rim of her mug. It splashed over her hand, but she barely noticed. She was too busy staring at Jake to see anything else around her. She gulped. How much of the conversation had he heard?

"Hi." He stood in the doorway looking better than any man had a right to in faded jeans and a worn gray T-shirt. The smile on his face told her he'd heard enough—if not everything. She bit back a groan. Just what she needed to brighten her morning. A man on an ego trip.

"Hey. What are you doing here?"

He held up a white paper sack with the logo of a local bakery on it. The expression on his face turned sheepish for a second before he shook his head. "I hope we're not interrupting anything. We brought breakfast."

We? She frowned. Before she had a chance to question anything, Miriam Storm pushed past her son into the office, wearing faded overalls and a blue baseball cap. "Good morning, ladies. Jake and I thought it would be nice to come over here and help you get the place painted."

Amber raised her eyebrows at Jake, who shrugged. She had to hold back a laugh. So it hadn't been his idea to show up unannounced. Why was she not surprised? He'd been roped into helping her. Good. Now Miriam would be on his case all the time. He'd never be able to get away from her. If anything, Miriam's involvement would only strengthen her plan and make things harder for Jake at the end.

Amber gave a fleeting thought to Miriam, who was like an aunt to her, and how she'd be hurt when Amber walked away from Jake, but there was nothing she could do about that. Jake himself had set this in motion years ago when he'd taken her virginity and left without a second glance. She'd hurt, for a long time. She couldn't help it now if what he'd done caused someone else pain.

"Jake, set those muffins down and get to work. This office isn't going to paint itself." Miriam made her way through the office to where Adele stood and picked up a clean paintbrush from the small pile Adele had dumped there a little while ago. "How are you ladies this morning? Beautiful day outside, isn't it?"

Without giving either of them a chance to answer, she grabbed Adele's hand and led her toward one of the small rooms off the back of the main office. "Adele, sweetheart, why don't we work out here and let Amber and Jake take care of the front room? Between the two of them, I think they can manage just fine."

Adele rolled her eyes, shrugged, and followed Miriam out of sight.

Once they were alone in the spacious main room of the office, Jake set the bag on the counter near the front door and walked over to where Amber stood, his expression apologetic. "Sorry. This wasn't my idea. And believe me, I tried like hell to talk her out of it."

"Yeah, I sort of figured that out. Your mother has the tenacity of a pit bull with a bone. Once she gets a hold of an idea, she doesn't let go, does she?"

"No. She doesn't." He laughed, but soon his expression turned serious. "You know what she's doing, don't you?"

Amber opened the bag and pulled out one of the muffins inside. Blueberry. Her favorite. She didn't indulge that often anymore, not since she'd spent two grueling years struggling to lose the extra weight and get down to a size eight, but once in a while wouldn't hurt.

She tore a small chunk off and popped it into her mouth, closing her eyes for a second to savor the flavor. When she opened them, she caught the troubled look on Jake's face and smiled. "Relax, Jake. You have nothing to worry about. Yes, I know exactly what she's trying to do, and I'm sorry. I can't help but think it's my fault, since I'm the one who asked her to set up the date in the first place."

"There's a big difference between a single date and what my mother thinks should happen here, between us. I don't know if you realize how serious she is about stuff like this. She's a psycho when it comes to this sort of thing. Obsessed with me and my siblings, you know, getting…"

She had to bite back the laughter threatening to burst from her throat. He stammered and sputtered and couldn't even manage to say the word. Typical man, allergic to any word relating to commitment. All she'd have to do was lean in close, press her lips to his ear, and whisper *marriage* to get him to turn tail and run. "You have nothing to worry about. I'm *really* not interested in marriage."

"You're not?"

"No." The word came out stronger than she intended. She brushed her hands down her thighs and took a breath before continuing. "I broke an engagement just before I moved here, and I need a little time before I look for anything serious."

Something she could have sworn was jealousy flashed across his gaze for a brief second before it was gone, replaced by curiosity. "What happened?"

She'd been asking herself that question for a long time. Zack was sweet. Very sexy. And an heir to a sizeable family fortune. He was everything she should want in a man, but he didn't ignite any sparks in her. She'd tried to force it for too long, and it had eventually had to end. She missed his friendship, though, more than anything.

"We just weren't compatible. We tried, but it didn't work out." Zack had been upset when she'd left. Upset enough to tell her he wasn't giving up on her. It had killed her to hurt him the way she had, but at the same time, she knew it was better to make the break now rather than a few years into a passionless marriage. The last thing she wanted was for him to resent her. She couldn't be what he wanted. He just had yet to see that.

"Why is this the first time I'm hearing about this? I would have thought it would have made it to me via the Storm-Velez grapevine in record time."

It was a depressing part of her life she'd rather not think about. She'd spent so much time making herself into someone new and had finally found she liked who she'd become. Zack should have been the perfect complement to her. But he wasn't. They just didn't fit, and the engagement had been a mistake.

"My mother knew I was seeing Zack, but I never mentioned the engagement to her. Does that tell you how uncertain I was about it, right from the start? I guess, deep down, I didn't want to get her hopes up over something that really shouldn't ever have happened. Want a muffin?" Suddenly uncomfortable and more than ready to change the subject, she pushed the bag across the counter until it bumped his hand.

He laughed. "No, thanks. I already ate. Being at my parents' house for breakfast—and to have a little discussion with my mother about what she can and can't do to manipulate me—is what got me into this in the first place." He made a sweeping gesture around the office with his hand.

"Not that I don't want to be here," he added quickly. "I have no problem helping out a friend."

"You just don't want to spend all Saturday hanging out with a bunch of women."

"Exactly." Relief flooded his expression. His smile showed off the dimples in his cheeks and made her heart hammer against her ribs. The pounding wouldn't stop, no matter how much she tried to ignore it, so she decided to change the subject to one that would remind her of what a dog the guy really was.

"So why aren't you married by now? I would have thought you and Shelly Rogers would have a big house full of kids."

Just the mention of Shelly's name made a lump form in her throat, even after thirteen years had passed. She tried to push old anger and resentment away, but couldn't quite manage it.

Jake paused. Nervousness passed across his gaze and he glanced around the room, his throat working as he swallowed, before he answered. "Shelly and I didn't last long."

"Big surprise there, knowing how you are. What happened?"

"I went to college in Boston. She went to Chicago. We grew apart."

So it had nothing to do with the fact that she was a vapid twit who couldn't string two words together to make a coherent sentence? Amber sighed. It probably had a lot more to do with that than he'd ever admit to her. It should have made her feel better, but for some reason, it didn't. "That's too bad. You made a cute couple. A lot cuter than we ever were, at least."

"I thought you said the past didn't bother you anymore?" The look he gave her warned her that it was time to shut up. To put the past aside, as she'd told him the night before she already had. And she had set it aside, for the most part. Some things still lingered, most of them involving Jake and the way things had ended between them. It was her fault really, for believing he cared about her the way she cared about him, and she'd learned to accept that a long time ago. She should have realized he'd only gotten caught up in the heat of the moment. She'd been as much at fault as he had for the way he'd walked away.

"It doesn't. It was just an observation." One she probably shouldn't have made so soon in the game, if his expression told her anything. She swallowed back the rest of what she wanted to say, and it left a bitter taste in her throat. Maybe she wasn't strong enough to pull this off, after all.

It really didn't matter if she was. She'd set it in motion, and the only thing she could do was see it through to the end.

She glanced down, and Jake was silent for a few minutes before he spoke again. When he did, the good nature was back in his voice. "Marriage isn't really my thing. I'm glad we're on the same page with this. You know how my mother can be. I try to ignore her, but it's hard sometimes. She can be a little overbearing."

She looked up at him, and couldn't help but laugh at the truth in the statement. Miriam had been ecstatic when Amber had asked her to set her up with Jake. She hadn't known the reasons Amber had wanted to see him again. Apparently she'd drawn her own conclusions.

"I know. Don't worry. I can handle her."

He stared at her for a long time, his gaze searching, before he shook his head. "I really hope you can."

"You're forgetting that my mother is just as bad as yours."

"That's true. She is." He brought his hand up to her cheek and brushed his finger down the line of her jaw. A shiver rippled through her. "Did I mention you look really cute today?"

Her face flamed. No, she didn't look cute. She looked as if she'd rolled out of bed and thrown on the first thing she'd grabbed out of her dresser—in the dark. If she'd known he'd be showing up, she might have worn something other than ratty cut-off jeans and one of the baggy T-shirts she usually slept in. "You're kidding, right?"

Her hair was piled into a messy ponytail, and though she'd washed her face, she'd forgone makeup since Adele had dragged her out of bed so early. At least she'd brushed her teeth. That was probably the only thing she had going for her at the moment.

"Nope. You look different than you did last night, but I like you like this. You look young. Sexy, in a college coed kind of way." He waggled his eyebrows and she couldn't help but laugh. Soon his gaze heated and her laughter died. Amazing that one look from him could turn her on in seconds flat.

She cursed her weak body. For too many years, she'd been reacting to Jake Storm that way. Like he was the only man who'd ever really do it for her. She'd had sex with other men. Plenty of them in the past thirteen years since her first time with Jake. The sex had always been better than her and Jake's bumbling attempt at eighteen, but for some reason she couldn't get him out of her head.

Probably because she'd never had any real closure on that part of her life. He'd walked away from her right afterward, and the next day, much to her surprise and hurt, had been dating someone else.

The thought of him with Shelly Rogers only strengthened her resolve. According to Adele, he'd spent the past few years since returning from law school doing to other women exactly what he'd done to Amber. He might seem nice, she might actually be starting to like the guy, but that didn't mean he got to get away with treating women like crap. Amber wasn't the only woman he'd walked away from. There had been many.

"What's the matter?" he asked. "You look so serious all of a sudden. Did I say something that upset you?"

"Nothing's the matter. It's early. I'm still not awake yet." She couldn't keep the hurt out of her voice and she glanced down, hoping he wouldn't see it reflected in her eyes. His sigh told her he'd seen it, and it only made her feel worse.

"Aw, Amber. I was a jerk. It just took me a while to realize it. I really am sorry. I never meant to hurt you, I just panicked." He leaned in and she forgot all about what she'd been thinking. His lips brushed hers in a kiss that was less caress and more small explosion.

His tongue dipped into her mouth to stroke against hers. Only their mouths touched, but it was a kiss she felt everywhere. Her panties dampened and her nipples hardened against her sports bra. He leaned in more, angling his head to deepen the kiss, and she sighed into his mouth. So last night hadn't been a fluke. If he was this good with just his mouth, how would he be with other parts of his body? She had a feeling he'd be better than the last time they were together.

A giggle caught in her throat and she broke the kiss. It was probably just as well. She didn't want to get carried away with Miriam and Adele so close. "This probably isn't a great idea."

"Why not?"

"Your mother is right in the other room. You don't want her getting the wrong idea, do you?"

He glanced over her shoulder toward the open doorway to the room his mother and Adele had disappeared into. "Probably not. If she saw me kissing you, she'd definitely get the wrong idea."

His gaze came back to hers and he smiled. "Then she'd never leave either of us alone."

Though he said the words, he leaned in and kissed her again.

The kiss this time was long and lingering and had her wanting to crawl inside his skin. He felt so good against her, but she had to remember nothing more intimate than kissing would happen between them right now. If it did, he wouldn't be the one to decide when and where it happened.

It certainly wouldn't be in her new office.

She should back away, but she didn't. She was enjoying it too much. Instead, she wrapped her arms around his neck and pulled him closer, desperate to feel him everywhere. His fingers closed over her hips and he squeezed, tugging her up against him.

Soon one of his hands came up to tunnel in her hair. He tilted her head back, deepening the kiss, before his lips left hers and trailed down her throat. Amber let her head drop back, a soft moan on her lips.

Yes, the man could kiss. Though she warned herself not to fall into it, she was loving every second of his touch. She splayed her hands across his chest, caressing him through the soft fabric of his worn shirt. He broke the kiss and hissed out a breath when her thumbs skimmed over his nipples.

His gaze snagged hers and the heat she found there made her breath catch in her throat. "If you keep touching me like that, Amber, we're both going to be in trouble."

He would be. She had enough control to be able to stop at the last second. At least she hoped she did.

She pasted on her sexiest, come-hither smile and licked her lips. "Maybe I don't care."

With a groan, he moved forward and sealed his lips over hers again, this time trapping her body between his and the counter. He left no space between them and she felt the bulge of his growing erection against her belly. She wriggled, earning another groan from him for her teasing. Men were so weak.

"Am I interrupting something?"

At the sound of Miriam's voice, Amber broke the kiss and pushed Jake away. Her face flamed and she spun around, leaning her arms on the counter. "No. Definitely not interrupting anything."

Not much, at least. She'd only been about to tear Jake's clothes off and have her way with him on the counter. Or the floor. Hell, even up against the wall would have been fine with her.

"It looked like I was." Miriam walked past Amber to Jake and patted his arm. "Regina and I have been waiting a long time for the two of you to figure out that you're meant to be together."

At the mention of her mother, Amber almost choked on the breath she'd been pulling in. They'd be waiting a hell of a lot longer if they thought anything serious could ever happen between her and Jake. She'd been serious about him once, but never again. She wouldn't give him the chance to hurt her any more than he already had. But they didn't know that. Didn't know what had happened between them because she'd been too ashamed to confess what she saw as a weakness. It was a secret she'd keep forever. No one else needed to know what had happened. Especially her mother and Miriam.

"You came over here to work, Jake. I suggest you pick up a paint brush. This office isn't going to paint itself," Miriam repeated her earlier words, handing him a clean brush. She gave Jake a nudge in the direction of the paint cans and turned her attention to Amber. "You have to keep on top of him all the time, or else he'll run wild. He never has been much for following the rules."

Amber held back a snort of laughter. "I'll make sure he doesn't get into any trouble."

As soon as Miriam left, Jake walked over and whispered in her ear. "I wouldn't mind you being on top of me all the time."

Her legs buckled and she let out a breath. Oh Lord, the man was potent. Keeping her distance was going to be harder than she'd first thought. She glanced up at him, fighting a smile. "Don't start. This is not the time, or the place, for that kind of talk."

"No?" He gave her a rakish smile that sent her heart hammering again. "Don't tell me you didn't think about it last night while you were alone in bed."

She'd thought about it, all right. So much that it had taken her hours to fall asleep. The fact that he knew it unsettled her.

"Your mother is right there," she hissed back.

"Yeah, so? She can't hear me."

"I absolutely can, Jacob Storm, and I expect you to get to work." Miriam clicked her tongue before she grabbed another paint can and walked out of the room.

Jake reached for Amber as soon as his mother was out of sight, but she backed away from his grasp, picking up the wet paintbrush she'd been using and brandishing it in front of her.

"Back off, mister, or you're going to be in trouble."

"What are you going to do? Spank me with it?"

She barely bit back a whimper. Damned if her whole body didn't go up in flames at the thought.

Chapter Three

Jake caught himself watching Amber out of the corner of his eye. Again. He'd been doing that so much during the day he'd managed to paint three light switches, a doorknob and a quarter of a window. The second he'd kissed her, his concentration had disappeared and he had yet to find it again.

Damn, she was beautiful. Sexy, too. Last night she'd been bent on teasing him. Her clothes and her attitude had told him that. Today she was just plain Amber, dressed in old clothes and painting walls, and still there was something innately sensual about her. The way her body moved as she stroked the brush along the wall. The way she bent over every so often for more paint. The way she sucked her lower lip into her mouth as if she were deep in thought.

It was enough to drive a man insane. He'd been semi-hard since the kisses they'd shared and he'd had to keep his back to her—and to his mother and Adele whenever they walked into the room. The last thing he needed was crap from them for his teenaged reaction.

He lifted the brush and stroked more of the paint on the wall, determined to keep his mind on the job he'd promised to do rather than the woman he'd rather be doing. The paint was light pink. He shook his head. Not a color he would have chosen, but he supposed it worked for a wedding planner's office. He could just imagine Amber filling the space with fragile white furniture and all kinds of flowers and perfume and lace. The thought was enough to give him hives.

"We're making decent progress," Amber said in a half-whisper, as if she was talking to herself as much as him. She didn't glance his way, but instead kept her gaze trained on the wall in front of her. She caught her lower lip between her teeth again and cocked her head to the side.

"Yeah. Between the four of us, we have this place pretty much knocked out." He finished the last brushstroke and set the brush down before lifting his arms over his head and stretching. "It'll need another coat tomorrow, once this has had a chance to dry."

Amber nodded. "Yeah, it will."

"Is Adele helping you?"

"No. She has plans with Max and the kids."

Perfect. His mother would be too busy on a Sunday afternoon to even think about painting. She'd planned to have the family over for Sunday dinner, and that wouldn't leave her time to think about much else. He wanted a little time to spend with Amber without prying eyes all around them.

"I could stop by in the afternoon if you want me to. I have to go to dinner at my parents' house, but I'm free for the rest of the day around two. If the two of us work together, we might be able to get most of the second coat on." It wouldn't take that long to slap a second coat on the office. If he could manage to keep his hands to himself.

Amber set her own brush down in the tray and glanced up at him, her expression coy. Her eyebrows rose and she scanned the room before looking back at him. "Are you sure you want to waste another day with me?"

He wanted to waste a day with her, all right, but not painting. He could think of many more things he would like to do, but he doubted she'd be receptive to them. She talked a good game, but the way she'd blushed when he'd whispered in her ear made him think she wasn't as bold as she wanted him to believe. The boldness was purely for his benefit, but he had to wonder at her motives.

"I like spending time with you." Always had. He'd always clicked with Amber, and late in their teen years, their friendship had turned into something more. But he'd fucked that up and he couldn't go back. He wanted to tell her how much he'd missed her, but she probably wouldn't appreciate the sentiment.

Instead, he decided to change the subject. Better keep things in the present or risk chasing her away. "Are you free tonight?"

"I was just going to get take-out and eat at home. Why?"

"Want some company?"

She regarded him through narrowed eyes. "What are you up to?"

"Nothing. I just want to be with you. We could go out if you want to."

"No. I'm too tired for that." She leaned against the closed front door—one of the few areas of wall space not covered in cotton-candy pink—and sighed. "Okay, you can come upstairs with me. But you need to behave. And keep your hands to yourself."

If she thought he was going to make a promise like that, she was out of her mind. "I'll try."

It was the best he could do. He'd been up almost all night the night before, going over and over in his head what had happened, both in the past and the present. He couldn't make sense of any of it. Something inside told him this was all too easy, that it should have been more of a struggle to get her to forgive him, but he pushed the thought aside. All he knew was that he wanted her. More now than he ever had. He wouldn't blame her if she hadn't forgiven him. Wouldn't care if she was trying to get back at him now in some way. He wasn't looking for forever, anyway. Just a good time for a while with a woman who fascinated him.

"You'll try?" She raised her eyebrows and her soft laugh filled the room around them. "Is that the best you can do?"

He took his time studying her, admiring every single inch of her. Yeah, even dressed in little more than pajamas she managed to turn him on. Upstairs, in her apartment—alone—all bets were off. "Under the circumstances, I'm afraid so."

œ œ œ

"I like what you've done with the place." Jake glanced around the small apartment, searching for the right words to describe his opinion of the place. "It's very…"

Feminine was what it was. Light yellow walls, lacy curtains and a floral patterned couch dominated the combination living room-dining room area. The stools at the breakfast bar in the kitchen were even delicate. He was afraid to touch anything. Afraid that if he sat on one of those stools, he might break it.

"Girly?" Amber asked. She shut and locked the door behind them.

"Yeah." He laughed. That was an apt description. *Girly.* The exact opposite of the clean, modern décor in his house. Amber's apartment, though small, had a homey feel he couldn't say he was entirely comfortable with. "When were you able to get all this done?"

He'd noticed one small moving truck at the beginning of the week, but hadn't seen Amber outside the building even once.

"I actually didn't do any of it. Your mother fixed it up after you moved out. All I did was move my clothes and personal things in and unpack them. For the past few days I really haven't left the apartment, since I couldn't sit still comfortably in here with boxes all over the place."

"She really changed it. It was so plain when I lived here. Everything was white." He'd lived in this apartment from the time he'd moved back home after law school until he'd bought his own house six months ago. The changes were almost surreal. It didn't even look like the same place he used to call home.

Amber pulled open a drawer in the kitchen and removed a handful of takeout menus. The selection in town wasn't huge, but she'd managed to snag a menu from every place that delivered in the few days she'd been around. She dropped the menus on the counter and started leafing through them.

"What do you want to eat?"

"Doesn't matter to me. What are you in the mood for?"

She shrugged. "Maybe pizza. Or Chinese food. Do you like either of those?"

He picked up a menu from the Chinese place down the block and opened it. "Do you cook?"

Her laugh was answer enough. "Why do you ask?"

"I've been back in town for a while now, and I don't think I have this many menus in my house."

"Well, no one's ever accused me of being a five-star chef."

"If I had to eat out so much, I'd get sick of it. You should come over sometime so I can cook for you."

Her eyes nearly bugged out of her head. "You cook? *You?*"

Why did she look so surprised? "Yeah. I like to, actually."

"I never would have figured. Mr. Jock, baseball player who never had to do anything for himself. You've become really self-sufficient." She glanced at the menu he was holding and shook her head. "So Chinese food is okay with you?"

"Yeah. It's fine. I'm easy."

Her raised eyebrows told him she caught the double meaning. "Good. I hope you like it spicy."

He didn't know why, but something in her voice made his cock stir. He liked it spicy, all right, but suddenly he wasn't thinking about food. He was thinking about Amber in her red dress and her killer heels. He bit back a groan and looked down at the ground. He'd promised her to try to keep his hands to himself, and here he was, five minutes into the date, and he just wanted to touch her everywhere.

"You look a little distracted."

Amber's observation drew his gaze back to hers and he shook his head. "Nah. I'm fine. Just hungry."

"Me, too." She smiled and reached out to snag the menu from his hands. "There's a notepad and a pen in that basket on the end of the counter. Why don't you grab it and we'll make a list of what we want to order?"

Ten minutes later, the list made and the food ordered, Jake pulled out his wallet and started to remove a couple of twenty dollar bills. Amber frowned. "What are you doing?"

"Paying for dinner. It was my idea."

"You paid last night. Tonight, it's my turn." She opened the fridge and grabbed a couple bottles of water, handing one to him. "Sorry. I don't have much else in the house. I really haven't had much chance to get to the grocery store yet. I'm still trying to get settled. Just finished unpacking yesterday morning."

"Water is fine." He twisted the cap off and took a long sip of the cool liquid. It went a long way to ease his parched throat. Whenever he was around her, his body was on high alert, and the fact that he couldn't seem to control himself unsettled him. Yeah, she was something to look at, but he had a sinking suspicion there was a lot more to his interest than just the way she looked. Part of him hoped there was, since he'd never wanted to be considered shallow, but another part wished there wasn't. The idea of getting involved with her on a deeper level made him a little queasy.

By the time he noticed what he was doing, he'd downed almost the entire bottle. With a shaky laugh, he set the bottle on the counter and slumped onto one of the stools.

"Are you okay?" Amusement laced Amber's tone. She took a sip from her own bottle and then swiped her fingers across her lips.

"I'm fine." *Just freakin' confused as all hell, with no hope of getting my head straight anytime soon.* She did this to him. Made him crazy. It had always been like this, and he'd always been trying to fight it, though for different reasons now than years ago. Back then, he'd been young and stupid and worried about his damned reputation. He and Amber had been on opposite ends of the social spectrum, and he'd been worried what his friends would think if they found out he was dating her. So he'd asked her to keep it a secret, and it had all blown up in his face. Now, he no longer cared what anyone thought, and she was beautiful and he didn't deserve her.

"You look shaken. All the flowers and lace are doing that to you, aren't they?"

He managed a weak laugh. It had less to do with the décor and more to do with the woman standing a few feet away. A woman he wanted to spend the whole night kissing and touching. Damn it, he wanted her under him, naked and moaning his name. At the same time he wanted to walk away before things got even more complicated than they already were.

His cock hardened against his zipper and he shifted on the chair. He was a mess. A giant, freakin' mess, and he needed to do something about it before his head exploded.

He couldn't, though. Not yet. He'd promised to try to keep his hands to himself, and as much as it killed him, he'd do it. For a little while. Once they'd eaten, he wouldn't be able to make any more promises.

"It's not so bad in here. I'm just tired. It was a long day."

She smiled, but it didn't quite reach her eyes. "Anytime you feel like telling me the truth, I'm right here to listen. We used to listen to each other all the time, Jake. I miss that."

He missed it, too. Missed having someone who wouldn't judge him, no matter what he confessed to her. He had his brothers now, and a circle of close friends, but there were some things he knew to keep to himself. Amber had been his best friend, and he hadn't even realized it until she was gone from his life.

Until he'd pushed her away.

He glanced at the countertop and let out a breath. "I miss it, too."

"So where do we go from here?" Her voice was soft and uncertain, and it made something hitch in the vicinity of his heart. *Shit.* He couldn't be falling for her again. Not this soon.

"I don't know. I guess we just take it one day at a time and see what happens." At least that way he'd be able to work on keeping an emotional distance. The woman who'd been his friend was gone, and in her place was a woman who threatened everything he loved about his life. He wouldn't let himself make the mistake of getting close to her all over again.

Twenty minutes later, they sat side by side at the counter, plates piled high with food. White food cartons lined the countertop in front of them. Amber had managed to find a bottle of wine her sister had given her when she'd moved back to town, and she poured two glasses. She handed him a glass and he took a sip, thankful to have something to do to distract him, but he'd never been much of a wine drinker. He tried not to wince at the too-sweet taste of the pinkish liquid—one of the trendy, fruit-laced concoctions.

"Sorry." Her expression told him she was holding back a laugh. "Adele loves this kind of crap. If it doesn't taste like fruit, she won't drink it."

He'd never had any kind of fruit that tasted like this. It was like drinking rancid berries. *Women.* He set the glass down and picked up a container of fried rice, piling a second helping onto his plate. At least he knew that tasted familiar, and it wouldn't kill him, either.

"Are you going to make it?"

"Yeah. Why wouldn't I?" He was a little out of his element here. If he had dinner with a woman, it was generally at a restaurant. The only time he spent time in a woman's apartment was if they were in bed. Amber seemed to be able to shake him on so many levels. He wanted so much with her. More than he'd wanted with other women. That was what scared him most of all.

"It won't kill you."

His gaze snapped to hers and he swallowed hard. Was she reading his mind again? He hoped to hell she wasn't. "What do you mean?"

"The wine. You're a beer guy, aren't you?"

The breath whooshed from his lungs. He forced a smile. So she hadn't been talking about commitment. Good. Because he had a feeling that commitment, especially with Amber, might actually be the death of him. At least the death of life as he knew it, and he wasn't willing to give that up. "Am I that obvious?"

"Yeah, you really are." She grinned. "I'll get you another water, you big baby, if you promise to stop looking like you're going to pass out."

"It's a deal."

ও ও ও

"Do you want to watch something else?"

Jake's gaze flew up to Amber's and his throat worked as he swallowed. His cheekbones were a little red and she couldn't help but smile at the sight. He was the one who'd suggested watching TV, but his eyes hadn't made it anywhere near the TV set yet. "What? Oh. No. This is fine."

"What's fine?"

"The show we're watching. It's...uh..." He glanced at the TV and back at her. "Sorry. I wasn't paying attention."

She tried to fight the smile that threatened, but couldn't quite manage it. He was cute when he was flustered, and he'd spent a good portion of the evening in that very state. Throughout the meal, he'd barely managed to relax. Only in the last few minutes had he really started to let his guard down. After they'd settled on the couch to watch TV, it had taken Amber about ten seconds to notice Jake's gaze wasn't on the television set. He'd been staring at her legs. His gaze drifted back there now, and she caught a hint of fatigue in his eyes. Poor guy. She'd worn him out with all the painting they'd done.

But he still couldn't keep his eyes off her body. She'd caught him staring often throughout the evening.

She pinched his side. Men and their one-track minds. "Would it help if I undressed?"

A slow, sexy smile spread over his lips. "You wouldn't mind?"

The only thing that saved him was his wink. If he hadn't let her know he was joking, she might have had to hurt him. She shook her head. "Not gonna happen tonight, Jake. I don't undress on a second date."

Though, at the moment, with his heated gaze all over her, it wouldn't take much persuasion. Just a few of the right words and she'd be all his. He knew it, too. She saw the truth in his eyes and it made her squirm.

"You sure about that?" It was more like he was asking for permission rather than doubting what she told him. Though she wanted to deny it, she nodded instead.

"Yeah."

"Can I at least kiss you, or is that against the rules?"

Every nerve in her body jumped for joy at his suggestion and it was all she could do to keep from grabbing him and pulling him to her. Or worse, tearing off her clothes and begging him to take her, rules and stuff be damned. All night she'd wanted his lips on hers again. What was the harm in a few kisses? "I guess one kiss would be fine. Just one, though. Okay?"

"I'm not making any promises."

He cupped her chin in his palm and leaned in to kiss her. It was just a brush of lips against lips at first. Soft and gentle. An exploratory kiss that didn't lead anywhere, and disappointment flashed through her. He started to pull away, but then brought his lips back to hers. This time the kiss was deeper. His free hand came to rest on her hip, giving it a squeeze, and her nipples hardened. His tongue played across the seam of her lips. When she parted them, he dipped it inside.

His fingers tangled in her hair and he tilted her head up, his lips leaving hers to trail a path of hot, open-mouth kisses down her throat to her collarbone. When he reached the neckline of her shirt, he glanced up at her, his gaze intense.

"You taste incredible. Have I ever told you that before?"

Her whole body responded to the harsh, raspy tone. "No. I don't think you've mentioned that."

"It's the truth. You taste amazing. *Feel* amazing. God, I don't think I can keep my hands off you."

"So don't."

"Don't tease me."

"I'm not. I want your hands on me." She'd never wanted anything more. She reached for him and wrapped her arms around his neck. "I don't want you to stop yet, Jake. Soon, just not right now."

He stilled, so close but not quite close enough. His shoulders heaved with his breaths. "You're asking a lot of me."

"I know." Unable to help herself any longer, she brushed her lips across his jaw. "I'm sorry."

"Don't be. It's okay."

He sank against her, flattening her on her back on the couch. His lips continued to taste and tease and it wasn't long before he'd settled on top of her, his tongue ramming into her mouth. The feel of his weight on her brought back memories she'd rather forget, and she shoved them aside. It was too good to pass up, and she'd be stupid to let old memories ruin an incredible moment. She clutched at his shirt, trying to get him closer. Suddenly, the contact they shared wasn't nearly enough.

Jake shifted position, and then his hand somehow managed to find its way under her shirt. He caught her nipple between his thumb and finger and rolled the nub of flesh, sending a spark straight to her core. She cried out and arched her back, pushing her breast further into his grasp. The man knew exactly how to turn her on, and that frightened her more than anything had yet with him. He knew *her*, no matter how much she tried to deny it, and that prompted her to end the little make-out session. She broke the kiss and pushed at his chest. She needed space. A lot of it, and soon, or else she might forget about the plan all together and invite him to spend the night.

Jake flopped back against the couch, his head resting on the cushions. He closed his eyes for a brief second and sucked in a few sharp breaths. "What's wrong?"

"We shouldn't. This is getting out of hand."

"This is too soon, huh?"

She nodded.

Frustration passed across his gaze, but his smile was tender. "Okay. I understand."

"Do you?" Because she didn't. Something unexplainable was happening inside her, and though she tried to stop it, the feeling wouldn't go away. She didn't want to *like* Jake, not really. She wanted to get back at him for what he'd done to her and countless other women over the years.

"Yeah." His smile widened, reminding her of the playful half-smiles he'd shown often when they were teenagers. "I do."

"You're not used to this, are you?"

His brow furrowed. "Used to what?"

"Waiting."

He reached out and pulled her against him, tucking her close to his side. He dropped a kiss on the top of her head. "This isn't about what I'm used to, or what I want or need. You're worth the wait. It just took me way too long to realize it."

Crap. How friggin' lovely. Of all the things to say. The man certainly had a way with words. If she'd been a weaker woman, she would have melted into a puddle at his feet. As it was, a sigh caught in her throat and she had to swallow it back. On the surface, he was perfect. The most incredible man she'd ever met. She'd just have to keep reminding herself that he was far from perfect. His flaws far outweighed his good points.

She pulled away and stood, running a hand over her messy hair. "Don't start. Just don't say things like that, okay?"

Every time he did, her plan slipped further and further out of her grasp. It had been two dates. *Two dates,* and already she was starting to think about scrapping the plan and trying for a real relationship with the guy. Now *that* was a disaster waiting to happen.

"I wouldn't have said it if I didn't mean it." He stood and walked up behind her, putting his arms around her and dragging her back against his chest. She found herself sinking into the touch.

"You're not looking for a serious commitment, remember?" *Neither am I. I just want closure on what you did to me that summer after high school.* She just wanted her turn to walk away. "I don't want anything serious, either. We really shouldn't be talking like this. Things could get out of hand."

"I'm okay with that."

She stiffened. This could *not* be happening. She didn't want to be having this conversation with him at all, let alone so soon after meeting up with him again. Years ago, she would have given anything to hear the words he spoke to her tonight, but now she neither needed them nor wanted them.

"But if it's not what you want," he continued, stepping back and turning her around to face him. "I'm okay with that, too. We can keep things casual, if that's what makes you happy."

"It is. Casual is good."

Anything more would be supremely stupid. *Been there, done that, already have the T-shirt.*

He studied her gaze for what seemed like an eternity before he nodded. Resignation flashed across his eyes, but he smiled. "Okay. Casual it is, then. I should go now before things get even more awkward. Walk me to the door?"

"Okay."

He took her hand and led her toward the door, stopping and kissing her softly once they reached it. He pulled back, ran his finger down the side of her cheek, and shook his head. "I know you think I was uncomfortable tonight, and maybe I was a little, but I had fun. I like spending time with you."

"I had fun, too." Right up until a few minutes ago, when he'd started spouting off what could only be lies. Jake Storm didn't do commitment. She knew that. Every woman in town knew that. Why was he all of a sudden acting like some kind of lovesick teenager?

"Good. Sleep well. I'll call you later."

When he left, she leaned against the door and slid down to the floor. Falling for him all over again wasn't part of the plan. If she wasn't careful, the whole thing might crumble around her, leaving her in as much of a mess as she'd been in the last time she'd made the mistake of getting involved with him.

No way in hell would she let that happen.

She had to steel herself against him. Indulging in the physical pleasure he could offer her would be fine, as long as she could keep her heart out of the way. It might not be too daunting of a task. All she had to do was keep reminding herself he'd hurt her before. Badly.

And she'd have to forget that the man she now knew seemed to be nothing like the boy she remembered.

Chapter Four

Amber leafed through the scarves on the rack in the small but classy boutique, pulling out one here and there and holding it up to her face in front of a small, oval mirror positioned on the counter. The scent of soft, flowery perfume hung in the air. The fabrics were soft and silky and just the feel of them brought a smile to her face. Soft, yes, but no doubt strong, and she had plans for one of them. Now she just had to find the right one. The *perfect* one. When Jake saw the one she picked and realized what she had in mind, she wanted him to be shocked speechless. Then again, with what she had planned, a plain scrap of cotton would probably accomplish that.

Nearly giddy with excitement, she wrapped one of the scarves—a deep blue one—around her wrist and nodded. Yes, the silk would be plenty strong enough. Jake would never see it coming. He didn't want to wait to jump into bed with her. He'd made that—among other things—perfectly clear a few nights ago before he'd left her house. In all honesty, she didn't want to wait, either, but she wanted to do things her way. *Needed* to. She refused to give the man the upper hand, even for a second.

A little playtime in the bedroom would distract him from things he shouldn't be thinking, and serve as a reminder to her that she hadn't arranged the date with him to get him back into her life. It was just the opposite. She wanted him out, this time for good, and the only way she'd be able to manage that was to find a way to get some closure on their past relationship and the terrible way he'd left things between them.

For the past few days, she'd been thinking about what to do, brainstorming ways to put a little distance between them and yet still draw him in at the same time. It had taken some time, but finally an idea had hit her. Jake was a take-charge kind of guy, to the point it made him stiff and unyielding sometimes. He had to have his way, or he wasn't happy. For as long as she'd known him, he'd been that way. She was about to change that facet of his personality for good.

"Can I help you find something?"

Amber spun around and found herself standing in front of the woman from the restaurant. The skinny blonde one Jake had been staring at when he'd gotten upset. His friend's wife. Amber's face flamed and she put the scarves back on the rack.

Her irrational reaction to seeing the woman made her giggle. The other woman wouldn't have any clue what Amber planned to use the scarf for, but a tiny sliver of guilt worked its way into her gut anyway. "I'm looking for a certain one, though I'm not sure which just yet. I don't have anything specific in mind, but I'll know it when I see it."

"No problem. Let me know if you need any help." She started to walk away, but Amber called her back.

"Aren't you Jake's friend?"

The woman nodded. "Madison Caldwell. I saw you out with Jake last week."

She didn't say anything more, but curiosity laced her tone. Amber managed a smile. "He and I are old friends. We used to date…well, sort of…but that was a long time ago. Back in high school. Actually, I used to live here, and I just moved back to town recently. The other night, Jake and I were just catching up on old times since we haven't seen each other in a long while."

The bell above the door jingled as another customer walked in. Madison glanced toward the door and waved to the older woman who stepped inside. "Hi, Mrs. Riley. Let me know if I can help you with anything."

To Amber's surprise, Madison smiled when her gaze came back to Amber's. "You're Amber, right? You have to be."

"Jake has mentioned me?"

"Only once or twice…or probably more like a few hundred times over the years." Madison laughed and flicked her wrist. "You really meant a lot to him. I think he's missed you since you've been apart. He must be glad to have you back in town."

Amber's brow creased. That was interesting. All the time they'd been involved, first in friendship and then later in something more serious, he'd told her repeatedly that he'd rather keep their involvement a secret. He hadn't wanted his friends to know he was seeing the class geek. What had happened to change his mind?

Guilt had happened. It was the only explanation that made any sense. He felt guilty for the way he'd walked away from her, and had needed some way to assuage it. She'd always been told that confession was good for the soul.

What had he been saying? It couldn't all have been good. Things had never been perfect between them, and though she didn't fault him entirely for that, she placed a hefty dose of blame on his shoulders. "I'm surprised he mentioned me at all. What did he say?"

"Not much, really, just little things here and there. But little things add up. He might not have noticed, but I did. He cared about you. I know that much for a fact."

Yeah, right. "We grew apart. I hardly know him anymore. He isn't the same man he was. In fact, right now he's so different I hardly recognize him."

Madison stepped closer and leaned in, glancing around the small shop before whispering to Amber. "You're referring to the women he dates, right?"

At Amber's nod, she continued. "Believe me, I've heard all the rumors, too. Things aren't as bad as they sound. I know he wouldn't want this to get out, but he dates a lot. And that's all they are. Dates. He doesn't sleep around as much as everyone here seems to think. He's a great guy, and he deserves to be happy, but for some reason he keeps sabotaging his own happiness."

Once upon a time, Amber had thought the guy was pretty great too, but he'd managed to change her opinion in a single night. "What do you mean?"

"He dates the wrong women. Idiots who couldn't even form a coherent sentence if you gave them all the words. They don't hold his interest for more than a night or two, but I think he knows that. The way I see it is he picks that kind of woman on purpose, knowing he could never get serious about any of them."

Amber leaned back against the counter and blew out a breath. Madison's words were insightful—and troubling. If what she said was true, it might change Amber's entire plan. "Why would he do that?"

"He's been hurt before. Badly, from what I can tell, and he's scared to make a commitment again, so he's come to the ridiculous conclusion that he's not ever going to get involved deeply with anyone. Have you ever heard of anything so silly?"

Amber managed a weak laugh. Yeah, she'd heard something like that before. She'd been living by that credo for years. She'd almost broken it once, with Zack, but had chickened out and ended the engagement. "That's nuts."

"My thoughts exactly. When I saw the two of you together and saw how content he looked, I finally began to have a little hope that Jake could find some real happiness in his life instead of spending all his time running from it."

Amber fought the urge to roll her eyes. Jake had a real cheerleader in his friend Madison. The other woman was wrong about one thing, though. He might find real happiness somewhere down the road, but it wouldn't be with her.

Amber straightened. "I have to confess, when he got so upset in the restaurant, I thought you and he had something going on."

"Not hardly. We're friends. At least we used to be, until Steve… Now everything's a huge mess and I don't know which way is up anymore." Her voice trailed off and she glanced around before dropping her tone to a whisper. "Did Jake think I was on a date?"

"Yeah. That's what I assumed, too. You weren't?"

Her soft laugh filled the room. She shook her head. "Of course Jake would think that. Typical man, always jumping to the wrong conclusions without asking questions first. I would have thought he knew me better than that. I'm not the one who wanted the divorce. The man I was with is my uncle. My mother's brother, visiting from Canada. I guess it's a good thing Jake thought what he did, though. Maybe it'll get back to Steve and he'll get jealous. I swear, I need to find *something* to give the guy a kick in the pants here."

Amber crossed her arms over her chest. Jake had made it sound like both parties wanted the divorce, but Madison didn't sound like a woman ready to get out of a bad marriage. She sounded like a woman who missed her husband and wanted him back. What hadn't Jake told her? "Why do you want him to be jealous if you're getting a divorce?"

She shrugged. Her eyes glazed for a second, but she swiped the moisture away with the back of her hand. She smiled, but the expression wavered and soon it fell from her face. "Sorry. This is a really emotional subject for me. *I* never wanted the divorce. It was Steve's idea. He got scared, or found someone else, or something. I don't know. He never really explained it to me.

"One day things were fine, we were married and he seemed happy about it, and the next he was telling me he needed his space.

That he couldn't be with me anymore until he had a chance to be by himself. I don't even know what the hell that means, except he's willing to throw away seven years of what I'd always thought was a really good thing just so he can have a little alone time."

Amber narrowed her eyes. *Men.* They were all alike. Pigs who thought women meant nothing but a temporary distraction. As soon as something better came along, they moved on without even a second glance. Hot anger swelled in Amber's gut, and somehow she managed to direct all that anger toward Jake. Or most of it, at least. "But you still love him, don't you?"

"Yeah. I don't know why, since he doesn't want to be with me anymore. I mean, here I am, having wasted so many years on a man who suddenly can't stand the sight of me, and I can't let it go. He told me he's finished, and I still keep hoping he'll change his mind. I should know better, though, right? He filed the papers. That should be enough to tell me he can't wait to get out of the marriage."

Amber made a mental note to talk to Jake about all this later. Madison's story sounded vastly different from what he'd told her, or at least how she'd interpreted it. The woman didn't look at all happy about her husband walking out on her, but Jake had made it sound like a mutual decision to split up.

"I'm sorry." Madison forced a smile. "You've come in here to shop and I'm dumping all my problems on you. I barely even know you."

"I don't mind. I'm a good listener." A listener who'd been passed over by a man, the same painful way Madison had. She, of all people, understood what the woman was going through.

"Thanks, but I really should stop talking about this, anyway. I do have a job to do." Madison reached around Amber and pulled a scarf off the rack. "The green in this one matches your eyes. I don't know what color outfit you want it to go with, but this one would look really nice."

Amber glanced at the scarf, a cream-colored one with a green and blue floral pattern, and immediately dismissed it. Not one she would have picked for herself, though it was pretty. She shook her head. Jake was too fair. The cream color wouldn't look good with his skin. She wasn't really worried about it matching *her* eyes. She picked up a bright, bold one instead, patterned with reds and oranges. A bold color for a bold act. A smile crept up the corners of her lips. That would work much better.

"I told you I'd know it when I found it. I think I'll go with this one instead."

Madison nodded in agreement. "Sure. That one will look great, too. Red would be amazing with your skin tone and your dark hair."

Jake's, too. She bit back a laugh. The bright color would catch his attention right away and make things even more interesting.

She brought the scarf to the register and paid for her purchase, still determined to find out what was going on between Madison and Steve. A firm believer in fairy-tale endings, Amber had made a career out of seeing people's dreams come true. She might not be interested in marriage herself, but that didn't mean she didn't want anyone to be happy. On the contrary, she'd prefer to see every married couple live happily every after, Madison looked about as miserable as a woman could get, and as far as Amber was concerned, that just wasn't acceptable.

When Madison handed her back the change, Amber smiled. "Men are pigs, huh?"

"What do you mean?"

Don't even get me started. She could go on for days. "Did Jake ever tell you why we stopped talking?"

"No. He never mentioned why, just said that you two grew apart when you went away to different colleges."

A lump formed in Amber's throat. That was the exact reason Jake had given her for his breakup with Shelly Rogers. So he'd given her the same generic explanation he'd given Madison for the way he'd left. Why was she not surprised?

"That *so* isn't what happened." The instant the words left her mouth, she wished she could pull them back. It wasn't like her to get emotional, especially around someone she barely knew. Then again, maybe it wouldn't be such a bad thing to have a friend around here. She'd never had many besides Jake and his sisters growing up, and since moving back to town the only people she'd really seen had been Adele and Jake's sister, Amanda. When she'd been in school, her appearance and her shyness had alienated her from most of the other kids. Now that she'd outgrown the shyness, it would be nice to have a few friends in Lilton besides the ones she considered her extended family.

"No?" Madison cocked her head to the side, a tiny smile on her lips. "I figured that sounded like too simplistic of an explanation."

"Believe me. It is." Her mood had taken a sour turn and she slumped against the counter. All these years she'd hoped, despite the way Jake had left her, that she meant something to him beyond being just another woman to warm his bed. Meeting up with him again, talking with him about the past and seeing how much he seemed to have changed, had reinforced that assumption—but now she realized everything he'd said to her since she'd been back in town might well be lies.

"I'm sorry. I didn't mean to upset you," Madison said. "You're right, you know. Men really are pigs."

"Definitely. Amanda and I are going out to dinner. Do you want to come with us? We can commiserate over margaritas."

Madison looked unsure at first, but finally she nodded. "Okay. I guess that would be fun."

Fun? Possibly. Interesting would be more like it. It had been a while since she'd had a great male-bashing session, and she had a feeling Madison would need it even more than Amber and Amanda would.

જી જી જી

The sounds of the cheering crowd blared from the baseball game on the wide-screen TV. Jake had settled onto his couch an hour ago and was trying his hardest to concentrate, but couldn't quite manage it tonight. His mind was on other things—things that didn't involve baseball. He had yet to hear from Amber, and he didn't know whether to be worried or pissed off.

It had been almost a week now since he'd seen her last. He'd spoken to her briefly a few nights ago, when he'd finally broken down and called her after she hadn't contacted him. She'd told him she would be too busy to see him for a few more days and to be patient with her, so he hadn't called again, but he'd expected her to. She hadn't, and it was eating him up inside.

His stomach clenched and his mouth went dry. What if she didn't want to see him again? What if this was her way of brushing him off, like he'd done to her so long ago?

He pushed the thoughts aside. Like it should even matter if she didn't want to see him anymore. She was probably scared of getting too close to him, and she had a right to be. What the hell had he been thinking, spouting off all that crap about commitment and her being worth the wait? He might as well have gotten down on one knee and pledged his undying love for her, twisted sap he was suddenly turning out to be. He hadn't meant what he'd said. At least he hoped to hell he hadn't. Commitment wasn't part of his long-term plan.

It was the wine she'd given him. Had to be. He couldn't think of any other reasonable explanation. The fruity, sweet wine had turned his stomach at the first sip. His system wasn't used to that kind of thing and it hadn't affected him well.

His brother, Brian, settled next to him on the couch and handed Jake an open bottle of beer. Jake took a long pull from the bottle and let the cool liquid slide down his throat. That was more like it. A ball game and a bottle of beer. Real men didn't drink fruity wine.

"Something bothering you?" Brian asked. "I don't think you've seen a second of the game. Where are you tonight?"

Jake shrugged.

"It's Amber, isn't it?"

So what if it is? Jake ignored his brother and turned his attention back to the game. Here it was, Sunday afternoon, and she *hadn't called.* Four days, and nothing. Why the hell shouldn't he be pissed off? He slammed his beer onto the coffee table.

"Jesus, Jake. Chill out. You're nuts. She's nothing to get worked up over."

That was what he kept trying to tell himself, but so far, none of his mental pep talks had accomplished anything. She was everything to get worked up over and she was dragging him around. Playing some kind of sick little cat and mouse game with his mind and his emotions. That should have been enough to send him walking in the other direction, but for some reason, he still couldn't let go. The more she brushed him aside, the more he wanted to get even closer to her. It didn't make any sense.

"She's different. You don't even know."

"Actually, I do." Brian laughed. "You can have any woman you want. Hell, you *do* have any woman you want. All the time. Why is Amber suddenly on your mind so much? Does this have something to do with that date she and Mom arranged?"

"No." He flopped back against the couch cushions and closed his eyes, pinching the bridge of his nose between his thumb and forefinger. A few deep breaths later, he dropped his hand. "I don't know what it's all about, but that date is the least of my worries. Have you seen her lately? You haven't since she's been back in town, have you?"

"No. Why?"

"Because she's freakin' amazing. Smokin' body. She could have any guy she wants." And apparently, that guy wasn't him. Two dates and she'd given up. Two dates and a hot make-out session, and she hadn't even bothered to call.

The irony didn't escape him. He'd done something similar to her not long ago. *Now you really know how it feels.* Except he didn't. It wasn't exactly the same. What he'd done to her, what he'd taken from her, had been so much worse. He couldn't expect what she'd said to be the truth. There was no way she was over it, and he'd been stupid to believe otherwise.

"Yeah, right. Plain, chubby Amber? Amber who never said two words to anybody? You don't really expect me to believe she's changed that much, do you?"

Jake nodded. If Brian had seen her, he'd understand. Hell, he'd probably be drooling after her, too. They'd always had similar taste in women. Amber wasn't really Brian's type, which settled Jake's stomach. A little. Brian was into long-term relationships, though Jake had yet to figure out what the appeal was. The way he saw it, tying yourself to another person for your whole life could only lead to trouble. Sure, his sister Rachel and her husband had managed it so far, though they'd only been married for less than six months. Steve and Madison, plus Amanda and her three weddings and a recent near miss convinced him marriage wasn't for him. Or for most people. Marriage was…unnecessary.

"She's not chubby anymore." Though, to him, she'd never really been plain. On the outside, she hadn't been beautiful, but her mind had been amazing. She was sharp and witty once she trusted someone enough to open up to them. He just hadn't been able to admit to his friends that he wasn't as shallow as he'd led everyone to believe. "She's thin, but she has these amazing curves. Even her hair is incredible now. Soft and silky and…"

He let his voice trail off, knowing he was starting to sound like a lovesick sap. He wasn't in love with her. Couldn't be after reconnecting with her only about a week ago. She drew him in and infatuated him. There was nothing more to it than that.

"Uh, you're starting to scare me." Brian leaned back against the couch and shook his head. "Since when do you wax poetic about a woman's hair? Last time I checked, you couldn't even remember half of their names a week after you dump them. What's going on with you? Is there something you're not telling me?"

A lot. Even now, there were things his closest friends and family didn't know about him. No one would know it from looking at the women he dated, but he preferred a woman to have a little substance. If she didn't have a brain in her head, he couldn't get himself interested for more than a night or two. Rachel would tell him he was setting himself up for failure by purposely dating the wrong women, but then again, she'd always been too insightful for her own good.

He picked up his beer again and downed half the bottle.

"Do you really think it's a good idea to get involved with her again?" Brian continued, digging in deeper when Jake just wanted him to shut the hell up. "After what happened last time, you know."

Brian was the only one Jake had trusted with what had happened between him and Amber, but sometimes he wished he hadn't said a word. He'd suffered through years of relentless teasing for his taste in women, and now this. He knew he was screwed up. He didn't need constant reminders. "She says she's over the past."

"And you believe that? Come on. You can't be that stupid. She's a woman. A Velez woman, no less. You know how they think. Just like Mom, and Rachel and Amanda. They can't let go of grudges. She's got to be setting you up for something here. It's never this easy."

"I know." He'd thought of it a hundred times since their first date, and was reasonably sure that was exactly what she was doing. Setting him up, trying to get revenge for what he'd done to her years ago. Problem was a huge part of him didn't even care. He still wanted to spend time with her. "I can't help it. I want to walk away, but damn it, I can't."

They lapsed into silence for a few minutes. The opposing team scored a double and Jake let out a half-hearted jeer. How fitting that the Sox were losing, today of all days. It only worsened his mood. It had been years since he'd let himself get tied up in knots over a woman. That had only happened to him once before. Ironic, but it was the same woman both times. Maybe that meant something.

He snorted. Even if it did, it was something he refused to think about. It had no part in his life, now or ever.

"You were in love with her then, weren't you?" Brian asked once the game went to a commercial.

Jake tried to deny it, but the words stuck in his throat. Instead of speaking, he polished off the rest of the beer, set the bottle on the floor next to the couch, and flopped back against the couch cushions again. Hell yes, he'd been in love with her. He wouldn't have slept with her otherwise. Now he might not be as discriminating, but back then he had been. Amber had meant something to him. She'd meant everything to him. And that was what scared Jake most of all.

Brian said nothing, and after a little while, the silence grated on Jake's nerves. "So what if I was in love with her. Would that make a difference now?"

Brian laughed, and it irritated Jake even more than the silence had. "I don't know. I don't get one thing, though. If you loved her, why did you walk away from her?"

To this day, he had yet to come up with a logical reason. He had plenty of reasons, and he'd stuck by them through the years, but they were flimsy at best. They had nothing in common. They were getting ready to go away to different colleges. His friends wouldn't approve. His family would read too much into it.

The reasons had all seemed valid at the time, but now he realized they were tenuous, at best. He didn't have a real reason for walking away, except that he'd been a coward. Maybe he still was, hanging onto old memories.

"I was young."

"And stupid."

"Thanks for reminding me."

"What? I only speak the truth." The amusement in Brian's eyes made Jake narrow his own.

He glared at Brian for a few seconds before closing his eyes. What the hell was he thinking, getting involved with a woman who probably wanted to screw him over? This was nuts. She was out to get him. He was almost sure of it, but he couldn't seem to make himself back off. If he didn't, he was setting himself up to get hurt.

Maybe Rachel was right. Yet again. Maybe this was the way his subconscious had chosen to finally purge him of the guilt he should have let go of a long time ago.

Brian was silent for a few minutes before he spoke again, this time in a low, quiet voice. "You don't want to fall for this woman all over again. That would be trouble, Jake. Big trouble."

Jake glanced at his brother through slitted eyes. *Thank you, oh, great master of the obvious.* "No shit."

He wouldn't let himself fall for her. Not any further than he already had. He could enjoy being with her, with the ultimate goal of getting her between the sheets again, but he wouldn't let himself fall for her like he had before. He didn't need her coming in and threatening his bachelorhood—a way of life he'd become very comfortable in.

"I won't," he continued. "That's not part of the plan."

"How can you be so sure?"

"She's already told me she doesn't want anything to do with marriage."

"Bullshit. The woman is a wedding planner. And any woman who says she isn't looking for marriage is a liar. It's biological. Women are the nesters. They want to settle down with a man and build a life together. It's just the way it is."

Not in his experience. He'd found plenty of women looking for a night or two of sweaty, no-strings-attached sex. That was *all* he'd been looking for since moving back home after college. He'd met a few women who refused to let go, but for the most part they'd wanted the same thing he did. Sex. And that was all. He hadn't even spoken to a woman about marriage in too long to remember.

"She just broke an engagement before she moved back here. I think I'm safe." At least Amber wasn't after him for marriage, but she was after something else. Revenge, though he had no idea exactly what she had planned. The trick would be figuring out how to keep his distance so he didn't end up as hurt as she'd been when he'd walked away from her.

"We'll see." The tone in Brian's voice reminded Jake too much of Rachel's warnings, and his mother's recent words about his state of mind, and he winced.

He wouldn't get involved. At least not beyond the physical level. The kicker was he really enjoyed spending time with her. Even all these years later, he missed the easy friendship they'd always had until he'd screwed everything up. Maybe it was the friendship he wanted back. Maybe something else. He didn't know. There was one thing he did know, though.

He was in a hell of a lot of trouble.

Chapter Five

"Sorry I'm late." Amanda scooted into a chair next to Madison and set her purse on the high, round table. "How are you ladies tonight?"

"Terrific." Amber slid a glass toward the petite woman. "We ordered you a drink."

"Thanks. God, you have no idea how much I need this." She lifted the glass to her lips and took a long sip of the pale green liquid. She closed her eyes for a second and let out a sigh. "This place makes the best margaritas. I need this tonight, too. So much. It's been a long week. So, what's up? Did I miss anything important?"

"Not really," Amber said over the din of customers and clattering plates and flatware in the crowded restaurant. "We've just been commiserating over our man problems."

Amanda cocked her head to the side. "I knew you had man problems," she gestured to Madison with her chin, "but I didn't know you did."

Her gaze swung to Amber. "What haven't you told me yet?"

Um, just about everything. "There's not a heck of a lot to tell. I was engaged before I moved back here."

Amanda's eyes widened. "No way. To who? You never mentioned anything."

Because she hadn't wanted anyone to know in case things fell apart. They had. Deep down inside, she'd always known they would. "His name is Zack Morales. He's a really sweet guy, but there just wasn't any passion between us."

She needed that passion. In her opinion, everyone did. What was the point of spending the rest of your life with someone you only felt lukewarm about?

Madison shook her head, but Amanda smiled. "I had passion with all four of my fiancés. Look at how well that turned out." She snorted a laugh. "Passion is important, but so are a bunch of other things. Like compassion and understanding. Intellectual compatibility. There are too many factors that go into making a marriage successful. It's so hard to know you're making the right decision. That's why all of mine ended so badly—I'd chosen the wrong men. My Mr. Right radar is broken or something."

Even Madison laughed at that comment. "You'll find someone eventually."

Amanda shrugged. "I don't think I want to. At least not for a *really* long time. I've had two or three more marriages than most women get in a lifetime, so it's well past time for me to take a break. No more men."

"I don't blame you. Men suck." Madison took a sip of her own margarita before she set the glass on the table with a thump. "They really do. I never thought that until a few months ago, but my oh-so-wonderful husband managed to change that opinion. Steve and I have been together for ten years. Married for seven. Why does he decide now that he wants a divorce? It seems a little late to back out to me, but what do I know? *I* never fell out of love with *him*."

She sniffled a little and took another swallow of her drink.

"Do you really think he does want a divorce, or do you think something else is going on?" Amber asked her. She refused to believe Steve would change his mind about the marriage so quickly, when there were other ways to work out their problems.

"Don't know. Don't care. What am I supposed to do? Fight him over the whole thing every step of the way?" She leaned back in her chair and sighed. "You know, that's exactly what I feel like doing. I want to make every second of this mess hell for him. He deserves it for what he's putting me through."

"Oh, I get it now. This is a man-bashing night, huh?" Amanda laughed. "Cool. I haven't had a good one of those in a long time. Not since Ronny left me at the altar."

Madison rolled her eyes. "I thought you didn't even want to marry him in the first place."

"I didn't think I did, but he could have told me he didn't want to get married before we were standing in front of the minister. I would have gone through with it, just to save face. What's one more divorce on top of three already?" She snagged a handful of popcorn from the bowl in the center of the table and popped a kernel into her mouth, chewing before she answered. "My mother still blames me for the fiasco that day turned into, and for some reason, she's managed to blame my un-wedding for Rachel and Doug eloping to Vegas in December. Like it's my fault they were smart enough to avoid the amateur wedding planner from hell. How nuts is that?"

Amber laughed, and soon Madison joined in. Amber hadn't been to any of Amanda's weddings, but between the pictures and first-hand accounts she understood why Rachel had chosen to elope rather than let Miriam Storm plan her wedding. Miriam tended to go a little overboard, to put it lightly. With everything.

"Totally nuts," Amber agreed. "But knowing your mother as well as I do, I'm not surprised. She'd probably been looking forward to planning Rachel's wedding since the day your sister was born."

Madison sniffled. "Can we talk about something other than weddings for a little while? The impending divorce is still so fresh for me. I don't think I can take much more of this without breaking down."

"Oh, honey, I'm sorry," Amanda said. "I know a divorce seems like the end of the world, but trust the resident expert on this. It gets easier. You're lucky you stayed married so long. None of my marriages made it to the second year anniversary."

Amber snorted. And the woman was surprised by this? "That's because you married bums."

Amanda shrugged. "What can I say? I'm a sucker for a cute face and a sexy body. Like you're not. You had that mad crush on my brother for so long before you left for college. I guess he's a good-looking guy, but he has issues. Big ones."

"It was more than a crush."

Amanda and Madison stared at her for a long time, neither of them speaking. Finally, Madison shook her head. "What happened between the two of you? You never did tell me in the boutique. Jake swears up and down that you were just friends, but I'm thinking there has to be a lot more to it than he's willing to tell me."

It figured. Even now, all these years later, he still denied what had happened between them. *Just friends, my ass.* He'd all but told her he loved her. He might not have said the words, but that summer he'd shown her with his actions what he'd never dared to say. Was he that ashamed of what he'd felt he couldn't even come clean about it after all this time?

"We were *way* more than friends."

Amanda nearly choked on her drink. She set the glass down hard, sloshing liquid over the salted rim. "Hold on a second. Don't tell me you slept with him. That's not possible. Someone would have known. Neither one of you could have kept that a secret from everyone for so long."

Amber said nothing, but her face flamed. She glanced down at the table, but the damage was already done. They knew. They had to, because she couldn't hide her embarrassment.

Amanda let out a long, low whistle. "No way. No freakin' way. I had no idea."

As far as she knew, no one did. She hadn't told anyone, and she doubted Jake would admit to what had happened. He'd been the one with the reputation at stake, not Amber. He'd been the one to suggest they have a secret relationship rather than carrying on in public, where anyone could see them. At the time, naïve and in love, she'd readily agreed to whatever he wanted. Now the thought of keeping such a secret from everyone turned her stomach. What had been wrong inside her head to let her agree with such an asinine idea?

It didn't matter what had prodded her to make the decision, only that she had and now she had to live with the consequences. Teenagers did stupid things all the time, and she was no exception. She shrugged off the sour mood that threatened and took a piece of popcorn. No sense dwelling on the past. She wasn't that same fat, plain, insecure girl anymore. This time, she was the one with the upper hand. Not Jake.

"It was just one time—a big mistake, and then he moved on to Shelly Rogers." She was still bitter about it, though she really had no right to be. He'd never promised her forever, and they'd never made any real commitments. She'd been young and stupid, and had hoped things would work out when she should have been smart enough to know better.

She was smart enough now. She wasn't going to let him hurt her the same way again. Now it was her turn to show him what it felt like to be dumped.

"What a jerk. I can't believe he would do something like that. I always thought he was such a nice guy. You can't trust any of them.

Men suck," Madison repeated. "Steve and Jake, and all of them. We really should teach them a lesson."

A smile spread over Amber's face. That was what she'd been thinking all along. She glanced at Amanda before continuing. "That's what I've been trying to do with Jake. So far, it's working."

Amanda frowned. "What are you planning to do to my brother? Not that I don't think he deserves it, mind you, I just want to make sure you aren't planning to hurt him physically or anything. He might be an ass, but he's still my family."

Sometimes emotional pain far out-shadowed physical pain. Amber had no desire to hurt him physically. She just wanted to break his spirit and bring the guy to his knees.

"Once he's hooked, I'm going to walk away. That's all." She shrugged. "I know he's your brother, but he doesn't have a very good track record with women. He's been doing this for too long, and getting away with it, too. It isn't right. Someone needs to show him that he can't go on the way he has been."

Amanda surprised Amber by nodding. "That's true. When it comes to women, he's a pig. Rachel and I have been saying that all along. Finally, someone has the guts to stand up for what's right."

It wasn't a question of having the guts for it, but more one of momentum. Once she'd set the plan in motion, there wasn't much she could do to stop it short of chickening out, and there was no way she'd let that happen. She'd come too far to stop now.

Amber took a sip of her water, wishing it was something stronger but knowing that wouldn't be a good idea. Too many calories in a margarita and she hadn't been careful with her diet for a few weeks. If she didn't start watching what she ate again, she'd be the size of a bus in a month, and that was a place she'd promised herself she'd never go to again.

"You know what you need to do?" Amber told Madison. "You need to teach Steve a lesson, too. You need to make him really jealous. Make him see what he's missing. That'll show him."

Madison nodded. "You're right. But I don't know how to do that short of parading around in front of his apartment naked, and I don't see that going over very well. What do you suggest?"

Amanda tapped her fingers on the table excitedly. "I know exactly what you can do. You need to start seeing someone else. And you need to shove it in his face so he knows what you're doing. That's the only surefire way to get him going and make him see what a moron he's being."

"You think so? Do you really think that'll work?" Madison asked Amanda, her expression unsure.

"I don't think, I *know*. Trust me. I've been through this sort of thing more times than I can count on both hands. And since I've given up on men for, like, forever, I'm going to have to live vicariously through the two of you. So let's get planning."

૨૭ ૨૭ ૨૭

Amber got home a few hours later and pulled her car into her parking space at the back of the building. She switched off the engine and got out of the car, taking a deep breath of the warm spring air before she headed for the steps leading up to her apartment.

Exhaustion ate at her body as well as her mind. She bit back a yawn. All in all, it had been an eventful evening. Her initial impressions about Madison and Steve had been right—Madison wanted nothing to do with the divorce. Amber fumed silently. It wasn't Madison's fault she married a jerk. Yet another man who seemed like the perfect guy until a woman let her guard down and settled into the relationship. Why Madison wanted him back was beyond Amber. If any man had treated her that way, she would have walked away a long time ago.

Is that why you're dying to get back with Jake, even though he put you through hell that summer after high school?

She gave the little voice in her head a mental kick and grumbled for it to shut up. What was going on between her and Jake wasn't nearly the same thing. She was trying to get revenge for what he'd done, the same way she and Amanda had told Madison she needed to get revenge on her soon to be ex-husband. She had no interest in Jake Storm beyond how she could make him hurt when she walked away from him.

Liar.

With a shake of her head, she climbed the two flights of stairs to her door. And stopped short when she saw she wasn't alone.

Jake stood on her landing, his big body bathed in the yellow glow from the overhead light. He leaned against the railing, his expression unreadable. His jaw was set, his lips in a grim line, and his eyes seemed gray as stone in the pale light. Uh oh. The closer she got to him, the slower her steps got and the more uncertainty swelled in her throat. What did he want? And why did he look so…dangerous? This was a new side to him, and it made her shake everywhere, both from nerves and a healthy dose of lust. She swallowed hard. By the time she reached him, her heart pounded against her ribs.

She stopped in front of him, her keys in one hand and her purse clutched in the other. He didn't say anything, so she sucked in a fortifying breath before she spoke to him. "Um, hi."

"Um, hi yourself."

He still didn't smile, and the stony expression on his face made her gulp. She'd never seen this side of him before—the grown-up man as opposed to the boy she'd known—and it intimidated her, among other things. There was nothing easygoing or fun-loving about him now. Her legs shook, but not entirely from anxiety.

She swallowed hard. "What's going on?"

He shrugged—a simple act that tonight seemed anything but. "Been out?"

She nodded.

"Doing what?"

Now her eyes narrowed. What the hell did it matter to him? He wasn't her keeper. They'd been on all of two dates. That didn't give him the right to question where she'd been or what she'd been doing. "Having dinner."

"With who?"

The jealousy in his voice made her smile. So he wasn't trying to be domineering, he was just worried she'd been out with another man.

She could deal with that. In fact, she kind of liked the idea. Jealousy played right into the plans she had for him.

"With friends."

His gaze heated and turned hard around the edges. He shoved his hands into the pockets of his pants and shook his head. "Yeah, I kinda figured that part out already. Male friends or female friends?"

It was on the tip of her tongue to tell him she'd been out on a date, just to see how he'd react, but she couldn't go through with it. It was enough that he thought that. She didn't need to torture him any more. At least not yet. There was a fine line between hooking him and chasing him away, and she had a feeling she'd lose her balance if she wasn't careful. If she chased him away now, everything would be ruined. She hadn't come this far to mess it up.

She walked over to him and propped her hip on the railing next to him. "I don't see how that's any of your business."

"I'm making it my business."

"Oh, really? How do you plan on doing that?"

He said nothing, just continued to stare at her with that mix of aggravation and jealousy in his eyes, and she pushed away from the railing and made her way to the door. Enough was enough. If he was going to continue acting like a caveman, she wasn't going to sit back and take it. "You know what? Never mind. Go home, Jake. Call me when you've gotten over this proprietary crap."

She unlocked her door and started to step inside. Jake apparently didn't want to let her walk away from him so soon. He grabbed her arm, spun her around, and hauled her against him.

In the next second, his lips were on hers for a searing, scorching kiss that was more of a possession than a simple kiss. She felt it everywhere, from the top of her head to the tips of her toes and every single point in between. His lips crushed hers. His tongue played across the seam of her lips as he demanded entrance, and once she parted them, he plunged it inside.

Amazing that with one touch of his lips, he could make her forget about the plan. Forget about everything except wanting to drag him into her apartment to continue what he'd started. She curled her fingers in his shirt, desperate to pull him closer.

He backed her into the doorframe, his body pressing against hers as he devoured her with his mouth. Sparks shot from every place they touched and traveled through her body, making her skin tingle and all the blood rush from her head to places further south. Her nipples pebbled against the lace of her bra cups and her panties dampened. She whimpered and melted into the touch, any thought she might have given to pushing him away abandoning her. The only thing she could do was hang on for the ride and let him do as he wanted. The man was an expert, and it had been too long since she'd been kissed so thoroughly.

He cupped her breasts and she wound her arms around his neck, trying to pull him closer as his thumbs played across her peaked nipples. Her panties dampened even more and she was struggling for a full breath by the time he released her.

He broke the kiss but didn't step back far. "Invite me inside."

"I don't know if that's a good idea."

"I know it's not. It's a friggin' lousy idea. Probably the worst one I've ever had. Invite me in anyway."

"Jake…"

He leaned in to kiss her again, hard and fast this time, and it sparked right to her toes. At the moment, she couldn't deny him what she really wanted. She broke the kiss and stepped back into her apartment.

His expression fell, but she held out her hand.

"Are you coming in, or are you just going to stand out there all night?"

He searched her expression for an endless second before his shoulders relaxed. "Are you sure?"

She shouldn't be, but she was. She'd planned to wait, but she wanted him tonight. Nothing could change that. Not even the common sense that seemed to abandon her whenever he got within a few feet of her. What she felt for him hadn't changed. For the first time, she began to doubt her plans for revenge. Which one of them would end up hurting when she walked away?

She had a feeling it wouldn't be Jake.

"Yeah, I'm sure. Please, Jake. I want you to come inside tonight."

A lopsided, sexy grin broke across his face. "Okay. If you insist."

ଔ ଔ ଔ

Jake walked into the apartment and kicked the door closed. He turned around long enough to lock it behind them before grabbing

Amber, hauling her against him and kissing her. He'd never get enough of this. She felt so good. So right in his arms, and it jarred him.

He'd chased her.

He'd never done that with a woman before. Had never had to. Hell, he'd even sworn he wouldn't, but there he'd been when she got home, all but ready to beg for a second of her time. *Pathetic. Really fucking pathetic.* And he couldn't have stopped himself if he'd tried.

Her fingers scraped across his nipples and a jolt of lust speared his gut. If he didn't have her tonight, his balls would probably explode. He'd been waiting for her for so long, it felt like forever.

He'd been standing outside her apartment for nearly an hour and had just about given up when she'd pulled into the lot. Now that he had her in his arms, he didn't intend to let go. She'd jerked him around enough. Had her fun. Now it was time for both of them to start acting like adults.

He tunneled his fingers in the softness of her hair, tilting her head back so he could deepen the kiss. She was so soft and pliant against him, so damned responsive to even the slightest touch, and it made him crazy. He groaned into her mouth, needing to be closer to her. A lot closer.

Amber broke the contact and stepped away, her expression a good mix of smugness and lust. She wanted to believe she was in control, and he could deal with that. Hell, at the moment, she *was* in control. She had him by his dick, and she knew it. All she had to do was crook her finger and he'd come running.

He rolled his shoulders and let out a grunt. How the hell had he let this happen?

"Want a drink?" she asked. "I have some beer in the fridge."

"You drink beer?"

She shook her head. "You do, though."

He was sure her comment should have some significance, but at the moment, he couldn't focus on anything but that small waist and those full breasts. The toned legs he wanted wrapped around him while he thrust his cock into her. He wanted her so bad right now he could barely breath, and she was asking him if he wanted a beer? Not hardly.

"No. I don't want a drink."

"Then what do you want?" She smiled. Dropped her purse on the counter and toed off her sandals. Her legs were bare and smooth and he licked his lips. "Tell me, Jake. Why are you here? What is it you want from me?"

"I want you. Have since that first night in the restaurant. I can't sleep at night half the time. Can't think about anything else. Just you." He walked over to her and cupped her chin in his palm, leaning in for another kiss. He loved the taste of her, all warm and spicy and sweet. Couldn't get enough. Now he wanted more. He wanted everything.

He pulled back and leaned against the counter, trying to slow his racing heartbeat. At this rate, he'd be finished before they even started. Assuming Amber didn't send him packing yet again. "What do *you* want?"

"I want you to listen to me. I told you I would call you," she scolded. Amusement glinted in her eyes. She lifted her hand and traced the line of his jaw with the tip of her finger. When she reached his chin, he nipped at her. Amber laughed. "Impatient much?"

Not usually. He prided himself on being an easygoing guy, but Amber had managed to step in and change all that. She made him nuts, had him ready to pull his hair out. She'd seated herself so firmly in his mind he couldn't dislodge her, and she was always at the forefront of his thoughts. Now she expected him to be *patient*? No way in hell was that happening. "Hell yes, I'm impatient. When I see something I want, I usually just go for it. I don't wait well."

"So I've noticed." She turned around and lifted her hair off her neck, revealing the low-cut back of her dress. It tied behind her neck, but her back was completely bare until just above her rounded ass. She couldn't be wearing a bra under it. No way. His cock jumped to attention. "Help me unzip this, will you? I can't quite reach."

He groaned. She had to be kidding. There was no way she couldn't reach that. "You're killing me, Amber."

"That's not my intention, believe me. Unzip me, Jake."

She didn't have to ask him twice. He slid the zipper down, exposing bare, tantalizing skin covered in a sheer, dark pink triangle of underwear. *Shit.* She might as well not be wearing panties at all.

He pressed a kiss between her shoulder blades and smiled at her resulting shiver. "Just so I know, so we don't have any misunderstandings here, what are we doing? Am I just undressing you so you can change, or is this leading to something more?"

She laughed, and the sound played across his skin like a caress. "You tell me. You're the one who came over here, all but demanding I let you inside. I let you in. Now what are you going to do about it?"

He swallowed hard. His cock twitched against his zipper. He knew what he wanted to do about it. He wanted to tear the insubstantial panties off, push her against the wall, and shove himself into her. "What do you want me to do?"

She turned around and brushed her finger down the center of his chest, stopping just short of his fly. He arched his hips, trying to get her to lower her hand just a little, but she laughed instead. "Whatever you want. Anything."

"*Anything?*"

In response, Amber only nodded. She gave him a sexy smile before she turned and walked toward the bedroom. When she reached the doorway she stopped and untied the dress from around her neck, letting it fall from her shoulders. It slid down her body and hit the floor with a hiss of material. As if it hadn't even happened, she stepped out of it and disappeared into the darkness of the room.

"Are you coming, Jake?" she called out to him. "Or are you going to stand in the kitchen gaping all night? I have needs, you know, and if you can't take care of them, I'll have to deal with the problem myself."

Holy shit.

She really was trying to kill him. At least he'd die a happy man.

Chapter Six

Amber waited in the dark, her gaze on the open door. Jake had yet to follow. Had he chickened out? Changed his mind and decided he really didn't want her, after all?

A pathetic laugh bubbled up in her throat. Lord, she hoped not. Here she stood in her panties and nothing else. She'd taken a big chance in being so bold, and he hadn't even followed. Embarrassment heated her skin.

"Jake?" she called one more time, wishing the floor would open up and swallow her whole.

Just when she was about to give up on him, to throw on her bathrobe and stomp into the other room to kick him out, he appeared in the doorway. Silhouetted by the light coming from the main room of the apartment, he made her breath catch in her throat. He was a beautiful man, tall and strong and sexy enough to make her mouth water, even in jeans and a white button-down shirt. She'd waited so long for this moment without even realizing what she'd been waiting for.

He flicked the switch near the door and bathed the room in light.

"What are you doing?"

A smile lifted one corner of his lips. "I want to be able to see you. I want to see everything. You're so beautiful, standing there like that. I've never seen anything so sexy in my life. You take my breath away, Amber."

He walked over to her and cupped her breasts in his hands, lifting them up and pushing them together. At the same time, he leaned down and captured one of her nipples between his lips. A frisson of heat shot straight through to her center and she threaded her fingers in his hair, holding him to her.

He continued to suckle her until she squirmed, and then he moved on to give the other nipple the same treatment. By the time he stood and backed away a few steps, releasing his hold on her, she could barely stand on her own. Her whole body thrummed, more than ready for him, and he had yet to take off a single stitch of his clothing.

Her mind drifted to the scarf she'd bought and she smiled. Yes, tonight would be the perfect time to put that little prop into play. She started unbuttoning his shirt and, once she'd pushed it off his shoulders and dropped it to the floor, nudged him backward. He landed sitting on the mattress and he smiled up at her, his expression a little bit wary.

"What are you doing?"

"I want to see you, too. All of you. But right now I don't want you to see me. I've always heard that being unable to see heightens one's pleasure. I wonder if that's really true. You'll have to let me know."

He frowned, but she didn't answer his unspoken question. Instead, she moved to the dresser and pulled the bright red scarf out of the bag. She spun around and held it out in front of her. "Pretty, isn't it?"

Apprehension flashed across his eyes. "What are you going to do with that?"

Oh, Jake dear, you have no idea.

"Nothing much." She shimmied back over to the bed and dragged the silk across his bare chest. His small nipples hardened and his pec muscles jumped a little.

He hissed out a breath. "This might not be such a good idea. I don't think I have the patience for teasing tonight."

"Good. I don't plan on teasing you." *Not much, anyway.* She climbed on the bed behind him and draped the scarf over his eyes, tying it in place without giving him a chance to protest. Once she had the bow secured, she leaned in and kissed the spot where his neck met his shoulder. He stiffened, and she ran her tongue up the side of his neck.

He grunted. "This seems like teasing to me."

"Not teasing, really. I'm just trying to make you happy. Trust me. You'll like it." She crawled next to him and gave his shoulder a push. "Lay down, Jake, and let me have a little fun."

He did as she asked and she went to work unbuttoning his pants. Once she had them undone, he lifted his hips and she slid them down his legs. Soon she had all his clothes off and he lay before her gloriously naked. He was perfect. Toned and defined, as if he spent a lot of time in the gym keeping up his physique. Before, he'd been an eighteen year old with an eighteen-year-old's body. Now he was thirty-one, and he'd aged well. Very well. She traced the indentations of his six-pack.

His rock-solid cock rested flat against his stomach and she smiled, reaching out to run her finger from tip to base. It jumped under her touch.

"No teasing, remember."

"I didn't make any promises."

She looked at him, laying on her mattress in nothing but the red silk scarf, and she smiled. She'd been right. Bright red was the perfect color to complement his fair skin and dark hair. It was a striking contrast.

She straddled his thighs and ran her hands all over his chest, her thumbs scraping across his nipples. She leaned up and kissed him everywhere, licking his nipples just as she'd played her nails across them. She bit down gently on one and Jake groaned.

"You're trying to kill me, aren't you?"

She laughed. "When we were together before, it was way too short. I didn't get a chance to explore your body, so I'm going to take that chance now. I suggest you shut up and enjoy it."

For a second he stiffened and she worried he might protest, but then he relaxed and smiled. "You want to explore? Go right ahead, sweetheart. Who am I to stop you?"

She proceeded to do just that, kissing him all over, stopping here and there to get a taste of his skin. She brought her mouth to his and kissed him, snaking her tongue inside. The feeling of power she got from the act was such a rush her whole body ached for more. She wanted him inside her, and she'd have him there, but not until she finished what she'd been wanting to do for so long.

By the time she sat up and scooted down his body, his chest was heaving. He didn't say anything, and the tightness in his body told her he was fighting for control. She wrinkled her nose. Why was he fighting it? She wanted him to lose it. Wanted him powerless to her. She wanted to control his pleasure, but he didn't seem willing to totally give himself up to the idea.

She leaned down and pressed a kiss to the head of his cock. He arched his hips, bumping the tip against her lips. "Please."

She complied, parting her lips and slipping him inside. With every upstroke, she swirled her tongue over the head, reveling in the musky taste of him. Now she finally had him right where she wanted him, teetering on the edge, ready to fall at any second. Jake panted and writhed, his fingers threading in her hair to hold her in place.

Having this kind of power over a man was an incredible feeling. One she decided she truly enjoyed. It was almost sublime. Big, strong Jake Storm was at her mercy, practically begging her with his body to complete what she'd started. She planned to complete it, too. Planned to make him crazy with need for her. Only then would she be able to strip him raw.

"I'm close, Amber. Too close. You should stop before it's too late."

No way was she stopping now. She lifted her head long enough to answer him. "I'm not stopping, Jake."

"Yes, you are. It's too soon." He didn't give her a chance to finish. He ripped off the blindfold and sat up. In one motion, he managed to get her onto her back and settle himself on top of her. The only thing separating his cock from her sex was the thin, unsubstantial triangle of her panties, and every cell in her body cried out for more. She arched her hips against him and a jolt ran through her sex.

"What do you think you're doing?" she asked.

"If you want to play, that's fine. I don't mind. You just can't do it tonight. You had your fun. It's my turn now."

He didn't give her a chance to think about it, let alone protest his words. Before she could even speak, he'd pushed her arms above her head and pressed her wrists to the mattress, and like a man who knew exactly what he was doing, he tied them to the headboard with the scarf.

She fought against the bond, trying to get her arms free, but he'd tied it well. It wouldn't budge.

She squirmed. "This isn't funny, Jake. What did you do?"

"Nothing." He smiled. "Yet."

He moved to the end of the bed, lifting her hips so he could pull her panties off. He tossed them across the room and they hit the wall somewhere near the closet door.

The smile he gave her was nothing short of devilish. His hand splayed across her stomach for a few seconds before he moved his fingers lower, lower until he pressed one deep inside her. Her hips came off the bed and she moaned. Another finger soon joined the first and Amber closed her eyes, reveling in the feeling of being so full. He thrust his fingers in expert strokes, his thumb brushing lightly across her clit in a way that brought her right up to the edge of orgasm without letting her topple over. He kept her there, suspended, for what felt like an eternity before he pulled his hand out and moved away.

She whimpered. "Where are you going?"

"Nowhere. I'm just getting more comfortable. And I want to return the favor." He knelt between her legs, raised her hips and pressed his lips to her sex.

She tugged at the scarf holding her arms, but she didn't really want to be free. Not yet. It was the most incredible feeling, being helpless and having his mouth on her. She writhed and moaned, her inner muscles quivering at the warm, wet contact.

Jake was relentless, holding her close and eating at her until she couldn't take another second. Her body bowed, her inner muscles tightened, and she came. The orgasm roared through her and all she could do was buck and squirm while he continued to tease her with his lips and teeth and tongue.

When her body finally stilled, Jake let her go and untied her arms. She started to sit up, but he shook his head.

"Don't move. Stay right there. I'll be back in five seconds."

He stood long enough to pick up his pants, pull a condom packet out of the pocket, and sheathe himself. Then he joined her on the bed.

"I'm not going to last long this time," he told her as he settled himself between her thighs. Amber could only laugh. Her body opened, welcoming him as he slid inside.

"Believe me, that's not a problem."

His strokes were long, measured at first, but soon he grabbed her hips and tilted them up, increasing his pace. Amazingly, the new angle sent another round of quivers through her sex. She gripped his shoulders and closed her eyes, lost in the sensations of finally, *finally*, having Jake inside her again. She hadn't been able to enjoy it the first time, and she intended to make up for that now.

He dropped his lips to her neck, pressing a line of open-mouthed kisses there. His jagged breath was hot against her skin. He came with her name on his lips, stiffening before he collapsed on top of her, his mouth against her throat. She felt his lips curve into a smile, and she couldn't help but smile herself.

"Wow" she whispered into the silence.

"Yeah." Jake laughed softly. "I want to stay tonight. Will you let me?"

She should kick him out, tell him she'd gotten what she wanted and she was finished with him, but something inside her wouldn't let her ruin what had been an incredible evening. Instead, she found herself nodding. "Yes. I want you here with me."

ରେ ରେ ରେ

Sometime later, with Jake sound asleep next to her, Amber lay quietly in the darkness. She was still smiling. Hadn't stopped for the past hour. Probably more. She'd been right. This time had been much better than their first attempt. Jake was amazing in bed. He knew just how to touch her, just how to taste her to make her quiver. All she had to do was think about it and she got hot all over again.

They'd rested after the first time, and just when she'd started to fall asleep, he'd woken her up with kisses everywhere. He'd worn himself out, if his snores were any indication, and though she was exhausted, too, she hadn't quite managed to fall back to sleep. Her mind moved too fast, her thoughts racing too much for her to settle down.

She glanced over at him, squinting to see him through the darkness. Even sleeping he was a beautiful man. Her body thrummed from the treatment he'd given it. She ached in places she'd forgotten about, and yet she had to resist the urge to wake him and start all over again. Yes, she wanted him, but in the past few minutes she'd begun to see she had another, far more disturbing problem. She hadn't realized until tonight how much she really still cared about him.

She let out a sigh and turned to her side, facing away from him. It wouldn't help her cause to start thinking about him that way. She didn't want to care about him. She wanted to get back at him. Falling for the guy all over again had never been—and never would be—part of the plan.

Yeah, just keep telling yourself that. Maybe one of these days you'll really believe it.

She shook off the irritating little voice in her head and flopped to her stomach. She *did* believe it. Had to. She hadn't come this far for nothing. She was confusing the fact that the man was a veritable sex god with feelings she really didn't have. The fact he could make her come with a few touches to the right place had obviously scrambled her mind, because she'd made a promise to herself at the beginning and she intended to keep that promise. She wouldn't fall for him. Ever again. It was as simple as that.

Her plan was still in place. In fact, she had him hooked so now it was time to move on to phase two and up the ante. This was the last time he'd see her—at least in such an intimate way. She'd leave him, and he'd be left hurting and wondering what had happened. Wondering what he'd done wrong to chase her away. She'd never tell him the reasons, though. He didn't deserve to know.

She shivered and burrowed deeper under the blankets. For the first time since concocting her plan, guilt wedged in her gut. Why did the thought of walking out on him right now leave her cold?

It didn't matter. She couldn't back down now. She'd worked too hard to make this a reality.

And she wouldn't, *couldn't*, risk getting hurt all over again. It just wasn't going to happen. She had to walk away. She really had no other choice.

Chapter Seven

Jake rolled to his back on the soft mattress and cracked his eyes open. Bright sunlight filtered into the room through the open slats in the mini-blinds. He squinted against the glare and fought the urge to burrow further under the covers and go back to sleep for at least another day. It took him a few seconds to process where he was. Lacy curtains. Yellow walls. Frilly comforter. A feminine, spicy scent hanging in the air.

Amber's apartment.

He took a deep breath and his lungs filled with the scent that drove him crazy. His cock went hard, but it was his mind that troubled him. Things had finally slipped beyond his control, and he didn't see any way of going back. Last night had been cathartic, and somewhere along the way, he'd come to a realization.

He didn't want to be single anymore.

Not only did he not want to be single, but he wanted to do whatever he had to do to keep Amber in his life. Just thinking about her made him warm all over, and that killed him. How had she managed to work her way under his skin so deeply in such a short amount of time?

He blew out a breath. Didn't matter how she'd done it, only that she had, and now there was no going back. He just had to find a way to convince her she felt the same thing for him. He knew she did. He'd seen it in her eyes last night. But she was stubborn, probably the most stubborn woman he'd ever met, and the task before him wouldn't be an easy one. A smile spread over his face. No, it wouldn't be easy, but it would be fun.

He rolled to his side and stretched his arm out for her, but hit bare mattress. What the hell?

He pried his eyes open the rest of the way and found her side of the bed empty. Cold. She'd been gone for a while, and she'd even straightened up the covers on her side after she'd gotten out. His gut clenched. Where the hell was she?

Maybe making coffee. He pushed up, sat on the edge of the bed and scrubbed his hand down his face, fighting a yawn. No need to get worked up over something so simple. She hadn't left. Where would she go? She had to be in the kitchen. It was *her* apartment, damn it. She couldn't have walked out on him.

Once he'd managed to shake off some of the exhaustion bogging down his mind, he pulled on the jeans he'd dropped on the floor the night before. Leaving them unzipped, he made a pit stop in the bathroom to take care of business before he wandered down the hallway into the small kitchen. Once he found her, he planned to drag her back to bed until she admitted that walking out without even a word hadn't been a good idea. On the rare occasion he spent a whole night with a woman, he didn't like waking up alone.

"Amber?" he called out to her as he turned the corner into the kitchen, only to find it empty. Worry crept up the back of his neck.

His gaze flew to the pristine, white-tiled counter and the pink sheet of paper resting on it. She'd left him a note. A goddamned note. His hands balled into fists and anger tightened into a knot in his stomach. What had he expected? Declarations of undying love?

Yeah. Like that would ever happen. He'd known all along she would do this to him. She'd made her point, and though he knew it shouldn't bother him so much, it did. He'd been hoping things had changed between them since that first *blind* date. Hoping she would eventually see he was a changed man, and he couldn't apologize enough for what he'd done to her in the past. Apparently she wasn't as quick to forgive as he'd hoped.

On stiff legs, he walked over and grabbed the sheet of paper, crumpling it into a ball in his hand. Feeling marginally better, he smoothed the paper out and took a deep breath before reading her words. All four of them.

"Thanks for last night," he murmured. His face heated and he crumpled the paper back into the ball, tightening it in his fist before he chucked it across the room. It hit the kitchen window with an unsatisfying small ping of glass and slid into the sink.

Thanks for last night. The woman was going to be the death of him one of these days, probably sooner rather than later.

Part of him understood why she'd done what she had, but another part of him just got annoyed at the whole thing. Yes, he'd walked out on her after sleeping with her. Yes, it had been stupid. But he'd been eighteen. A high-school graduate for all of a month and getting ready to embark on a new path in life. He'd been a kid. They both had. They were adults now and her actions struck him as juvenile and more than a little aggravating.

With a heavy sigh, he walked over to the sink, grabbed the paper, and stuffed it into the trash. Two could play at this game. And he had a lot more practice.

Not feeling any better, Jake stalked back into the bedroom and started pulling on the rest of his clothes. Who the hell did she think she was, walking out on him? Like a friggin' *thank-you* note was supposed to make him feel any better.

It was more than he'd given her when he'd walked out on her.

He pushed the thought away, not wanting to be troubled by residual guilt right now. Thirteen freakin' years had passed. Neither of them were kids anymore. He wasn't going to let her get away with this.

Once he'd tied his shoes, he left the apartment and pounded down the flight of stairs to her office. He opened the door and let it slam against the wall, not caring if it did any damage. He didn't care about anything right now except finding Amber and laying into her for putting him through this shit.

When he glanced up, he found himself face to face with a whole shitload of women gaping at him with various degrees of humor in their eyes. His mother. Adele and Regina Velez. Amanda and Madison.

His gaze zeroed in on Amber. She hung back from the group, a smug look on her face and her eyebrows raised. Her arms were crossed over her chest and she shook her head, staring at him like he was a child who'd managed to annoy her. Maybe he *was* acting childish, but one juvenile turn deserved another. He narrowed his eyes.

"You. Outside. Now."

A quick burst of laughter escaped from her lips. Her expression turned incredulous. "Excuse me?"

"You heard me. Outside, Amber. Right now."

Someone snorted, and he had a sinking suspicion it was his mother. He didn't dare look at her, or any of them for that matter. If he caught any humor in their eyes, he'd lose his momentum. He needed that momentum right now to keep him from looking like too much of an ass.

Amber's gaze flashed fire. She dropped her hands to her hips and lifted her chin. "If you think you can talk to me like that, buddy, you'd better think again. Would you like to try that request again, only a little more nicely this time?"

He gave a fleeting thought to the fact he was acting like some sort of deranged caveman, but dismissed it almost as quickly as it came to him. So what if he was? It wasn't like he could stop himself. Asking nicely was out of the question. He was too far gone for that.

He blew out a breath and narrowed his eyes. "Do you want me to lift you over my shoulder and carry you outside?"

"Not especially."

Amanda snickered and Jake threw her a glare. He *so* didn't need outside involvement in his tirade, especially from Amanda of the four weddings. He was doing fine making a fool out of himself all on his own. Amber was calling his bluff, and part of him knew it was time to back away, but he refused to stop now. If he did, he'd look like even more of an ass than he did now, if that was even possible.

He made a snap decision and walked over to her, picking her up and swinging her over his shoulder. Amber let out a lewd curse and silence fell over the room. Jake didn't take time to look at any of the other women in the room. He didn't want to see their reactions, especially his mother's. She'd skin him alive later, and he was okay with that. Instead, he carried Amber out to the landing and pulled the door shut behind them.

Once alone, he set her on her feet.

She slammed her small fist into his shoulder. "What the hell were you thinking?"

Jake rubbed his arm. Man, she had a hell of a swing for such a little thing. "I was about to ask you the same thing."

"I don't have time for this. I have *work* to do. The office is opening this week and I still have a lot to get organized." She reached for the doorknob, but he stepped into her path. "Jake, get out of the way. Unlike some people, I take things seriously."

"I take things seriously. Very seriously. Especially when certain women walk away, thinking leaving me a fucking thank-you note would be a good idea."

She started to move past him, but stopped and put her hands on her hips. "Let me go back inside, Jake. We can talk about this later."

"We can talk about it now."

"No, thanks. I'm a little pissed off over you storming into my office and acting like King Kong. If you want to talk to me, you need to at least pretend you're civil."

He rolled his shoulders and took a breath. Civil was about as likely right now as getting an ice cube in hell. He took a breath, fighting for control that seemed to be eluding him. He usually prided himself in his ability to keep his emotions in check, but something about Amber made him lose it every time. "I'm trying."

"Try harder." She tapped her foot on the landing slats, her jaw set and the glint in her eyes hard. Damn, she was pissed. He'd never seen her this angry before. "I'm waiting."

Her full lips parted and her expression stern, he couldn't help but notice how sexy she looked when she was angry. Damn it, it turned him on a hell of a lot more than it should. How could she expect him to hold a normal conversation now? No freakin' way was this whole *civil* thing happening.

In one swift motion, he pulled her toward him and sealed his lips over hers.

She fought against the kiss for all of two seconds before her arms came around his neck. He dipped his tongue into her mouth and reveled in the taste of her. Toothpaste and coffee. She tasted like morning—a morning that should have been his, if she'd had the guts to stay in bed with him. She'd taken the coward's way out, though.

This morning would be the last time she'd do that. After today, he intended to do whatever he had to in order to keep her close, even if it meant keeping her awake all night long.

His hand tangled in her hair and he tilted her head to deepen the kiss. She moaned and pressed closer to him.

A whistle from the street below alerted him to where they were and he pulled away, panting.

"What do you think you're doing?" Amber's voice was barely above a whisper, but it dripped with aggravation.

"Kissing you. I thought you liked when I did that. You didn't seem to have any complaints last night."

"I do like it, but I don't like this barbaric attitude you've suddenly come down with. Knock it off, caveman."

He couldn't help but laugh, but the laugh died when he caught the look in her eyes. "Sorry."

She paced back and forth across the landing for a few seconds before she stopped and shook her head. "Are you really, or is that just something you're saying to get you out of trouble?"

Both. "I'm really sorry. I didn't mean to act like that, but after that incredible night I woke up alone and I guess I sort of freaked."

"Doesn't feel very good, does it?"

The hurt in her eyes tugged at something deep inside him. He'd been such a jerk to walk out on her. Plain or stunning, carrying a few extra pounds or slim, she was one hell of a woman and he might have screwed up the best thing that had ever happened to him. Guilt had eaten away at him for years, but he didn't see the full repercussions of his mistake until just this moment, looking at her and thinking he might have lost her for good. He reached for her, but she ducked away.

"Amber, please. Talk to me."

"I don't know if there's anything left to talk about. You should go home now. I really don't have time for this."

Even though she said the words, she made no move to get past him and go back into the office. She just stood there staring at him, as if waiting for him to protest. He closed his eyes for a second and let out a breath. When he opened them, she still hadn't moved. Curiosity played at the edges of her eyes.

What did she want from him? Was she looking for another apology? He didn't know what else he could say, what else he could do to convince her he truly was sorry. He'd said the words more times to her than he had to any other woman, and still she didn't seem to believe him. Enough was enough. It was time for them to both stop acting like children and start acting like the adults they were. She might hide behind her plans for revenge, but she felt something between them as much as he did. She could deny it all she wanted, and she would, but he caught a glimpse of it in her eyes whenever he looked at her.

"You've walked out on me like I walked out on you. You've had your revenge, done exactly what you've been planning to do. Do you feel better now?"

She seemed to contemplate his question for a few seconds, her lower lip caught between her teeth and her gaze heavenward, before she answered. "Actually, I do."

"Good. Have dinner with me tonight."

Her gaze flew to his and she frowned. "What?"

"We're even now, right?" God, he hoped so. He couldn't handle atoning for any more of his perceived sins. He just wanted to move past this, to move on with his life and to try to prove to her that she belonged in it. "I want to start over. To have dinner with you."

"You mean you want to take me to bed again. Why not skip dinner and just head straight for the bedroom? Don't bother spending your money. I'm easy, right? I think you managed to prove that last night as easily as you did thirteen years ago."

He scoffed. Easy? Was she kidding? She had to be the most difficult, complicated woman he'd ever met and he loved her all the more for it.

Fuck, no. He didn't *love* her. He liked her. A lot. But that was as far as it went. It was way too soon for anything even resembling love.

"No. That's not what I want. And if you're easy, then so am I. I didn't do anything to hold back."

"Yeah, but you're a guy. You're not supposed to have to."

Tears glistened in her eyes and his gut clenched. If he hadn't acted like such a moron, he wouldn't have made her cry. He'd *never* seen Amber cry. Ever. He didn't like it at all.

He cupped her chin in his palm and brushed her cheek with his thumb. She sniffled. Leaned into his touch for a second before her gaze hardened and she stepped back, swiping her hands across her eyes.

"This is a mess. Maybe we should just forget the whole thing. Stop seeing each other."

The woman had to be out of her friggin' mind to suggest something like that. "No."

She blinked at him. "No? Are you ordering me around again?"

"No. I'm just saying I'm not willing to give you up. I want to be with you."

"Really?" She hiccupped, but covered the small sound with a bitter laugh. "Seriously, Jake. I don't think it's a good idea. I'm not over the past as much as I thought."

"Me, either." It came out as little more than a whisper, but her gaze snapped to his and he knew she'd heard it.

"What do you mean?"

"Just what I said."

"It couldn't have meant to you what it did to me, Jake." Her eyes teared up again, and this time she didn't seem to want to fight it. The tears streamed down her cheeks and she let out a watery sigh. "I'd never been with anyone else. You were my first. To have you walk away devastated me."

"You were my first, too." The words slipped out before he had a chance to pull them back, but he hadn't really wanted to stop them. He'd never told her, but she had a right to know. Especially after all he'd put her through.

The tears stopped. She swiped her hands across her cheeks and shook her head. "No way. There's absolutely no way you could have made it all the way through high school without sleeping with someone. How is that even possible?"

Not knowing what to say, he sucked in a few breaths. He took a few seconds to gather his thoughts, rather than blurt out the first thing that came to mind. *I didn't want anyone else. I was in love with you.* "We were sort of seeing each other. I didn't think it would be right to have sex with anyone else, and I didn't want to push you."

"You've got to be kidding me. We never made any real commitment."

"I know." The whole situation had been impossibly complicated. On one hand, he'd wanted to make a commitment to her, on the other, he'd known it just wasn't possible.

"You dated other girls, Jake. I know you did."

"I went on dates. They didn't mean anything. What happened between us meant a lot to me. What's it going to take to get you to believe that?"

She said nothing for so long he was afraid she was going to walk away, but after a few minutes, she slumped against the railing and put her hands in the pockets of her shorts. "It couldn't have meant much if you were sleeping with Shelly a week later."

He bit back a groan. She'd made so many assumptions about him, and he'd never bothered to correct them. He could only imagine what she really thought of him. The idea brought up a bitter laugh. Time for yet another painful confession. He had to clear his throat before he could get his voice to work. "I never slept with Shelly."

"Like I'm supposed to believe that?"

"I didn't sleep with anyone else until college." And not for months into that. He'd been too shaken by the strength of his feelings for

Amber. Feelings he'd never really wanted but that had snuck up on him anyway. If things had been different, if they'd gone to the same school, his life wouldn't have turned out the way it had.

"Believe what you want, but I'm telling you the truth. I dated Shelly, but I had no interest in sleeping with her."

"Why not? She was beautiful."

Still is. She still didn't do anything for him. "Because she's a shallow airhead. I prefer smart women."

"Yeah, right."

"I do."

"Then why did you walk out on me?"

"Because you scared the crap out of me. You still do. Until you walked back into my life, I liked being single." Now the thought made the inside of his mouth as dry and rough as sandpaper. "You're here again, though, and I can't explain it, but things have changed. I just want to be with you."

The sadness and anger left her expression. She reached for him, wrapped her arms around his neck and pressed her cheek to his chest. They stood there like that, unmoving and silent, for what felt like forever.

When she finally pulled away, he asked her again. "Have dinner with me tonight. Please."

"Okay. I think we have a lot to discuss. But there's something I need you to do for me."

"What's that?"

"Have your friend Steve there. At least for a little while."

Her request made him raise his eyebrows. What did she have in mind?

"Can I ask why?" He said the words, but he wasn't sure if he really wanted the answer.

"You think he and Madison should get back together, right?"

"Yeah."

"So does she." She gestured with her chin toward the office door. "Even now, she's probably in there talking about him. She doesn't stop. She's angry with him for asking for the divorce, especially since he didn't give her a solid reason for wanting it."

"And what does having Steve come out to dinner with us have to do with any of this?"

"Trust me. I have a plan."

He laughed. He'd seen her plans in action and didn't care to have to live through another one. It would take a lot of convincing on her part to get him to go along with anything. "I'm not doing anything until you fill me in."

Amber rolled her eyes. "Okay, but you have to trust me on this. Think you can manage that?"

"It depends on what you have in mind."

A sly smile spread over her face. "Madison and I have been discussing this, and we need your help to pull this off. Here's what we need to do."

Chapter Eight

All eyes were on Amber when she stepped back into the office alone. Jake had begged off coming inside, saying he had a client appointment in an hour and needed to run home and shower and change first. Part of her was a little miffed he'd left her to deal with the aftermath of his ridiculous behavior alone, but another, larger part didn't mind so much. There would be enough questions, especially from her mother and Miriam. She didn't feel like fielding them with Jake standing next to her. Especially not after he'd pulled that caveman act, threatened her and practically dragged her out of the office—and she'd let him do it with minimal argument. How weak could a woman get?

She was still processing what he'd told her, and probably would be for a good long while. Jake had been a virgin, too? How had she not known that? It amazed her that she'd been his first. They'd been high-school graduates at the time, hanging around town with not much to do for the summer before they went off to college. Jake had always been popular. Why hadn't he had sex before that night things had gotten carried away between them? It couldn't be for the reason he'd given her. That just didn't make sense.

"What was that all about?" her mother asked, tearing Amber from her memories.

"Nothing much." Amber walked over to the corner and started unpacking one of the few remaining boxes. In the last week, with lots of help from her family and friends, she'd managed to get the office nearly set up. Only a few more last-minute details and she'd be able to open for business. The thought scared her as much as it excited her. Going into business for herself, being totally dependent on herself for income, sent a sliver of anxiety slicing through her gut. She'd put the opening off for as long as she could, but her savings would only go so far. It was well past time to stand on her own two feet. She did it in every other area of her life—why not this one, too?

"Do I hear wedding bells in the future?" her mother continued, her tone a little too hopeful. The words yanked Amber back to the present and she sighed.

In your dreams, maybe, but not in my reality. "I hope so. Lots of them. This is a wedding planner's office, so wedding bells are pretty good for business."

Her mother shook her head. "I mean you and Jake."

"We've been dating for a week."

"I know, but that doesn't always matter. You've known him much longer than that, and there's always been something between you."

Amber swung her gaze to her mother and tried to drain all the emotion from her expression. "There was never anything between us. We were friends."

In the past week, she'd come to accept that fact after believing for so many years they'd had more, but Jake's confession made her wonder. Confusion had become a normal part of her life since moving back home, and things got worse with every new fact she learned. Not that the past held much bearing over the future. It didn't. She didn't know what the future with Jake would hold, but for the first time since hooking up with him again, she was willing to find out.

"Everyone noticed." Her mother spoke in a singsong voice that grated on Amber's nerves.

"Great. That's just wonderful." Jake wouldn't like to hear that, since he'd wanted to keep it secret for so long. She shook her head and started leafing through the box, looking through the papers inside and organizing them into piles on the floor. "We're just dating. Don't read into it any more than that. We haven't made a commitment, and to be honest, I don't know if we will."

"Right." Her mother's snort of disbelief made Amber wince. What did the woman want from her? Amber didn't know what was going on with Jake. Couldn't figure it out, but she wouldn't be pushed into making decisions, either. If more happened, it would happen. If it didn't, she'd pick herself up and move on with her life. She cared about Jake, more now than she'd even realized, but she was done hurting because of him. She'd already survived enough of that particular pain in her life.

A few minutes later, Madison came up to her. She sat on the floor, crossed one leg over the other, and leaned toward Amber. "What happened?" she asked in a whisper.

"Nothing. It was just a misunderstanding."

"Yeah, of epic proportions."

"It wasn't as bad as it looked."

Time to change the subject. If Amber kept thinking about Jake, it would only depress her. As much as she wanted to shout out that she'd accomplished her goal, that she'd made him pay for the way he hurt her, the victory was empty. It hadn't felt as good to leave him as she'd thought it would. In fact, walking out had made her stomach ache. To make things worse, she hadn't stuck with the original plan to not see him again once she'd had her payback. She'd agreed to have dinner with him less than three hours after she'd walked out. That could only turn out to be a big, honking mistake, and if she ended up alone again she only had herself to blame.

"Hey, I wanted to talk to you about something. Are you busy tonight?" Amber asked.

"No. Why?"

"Make plans. With a man. Can you find someone to take out on such short notice?"

"I think so." Madison's expression turned suspicious. "What's going on?"

"Just trust me. Jake and I talked about your problem with Steve, and he wants to help. He's going to get Steve to Casey's Bar at six tonight. If you're there, he'll see you with someone else. Then he can see what it's like to be on the other end. To be the person not asking for space."

Madison's eyes widened and she licked her lips. For a second, Amber thought she'd chicken out, but finally she nodded. "Okay. I'll do it."

"Awesome." With any luck, it would be enough to get Steve to see what he'd be giving up if he went through with the divorce. According to Jake, Steve still loved Madison and was miserable without her, but had a stubborn streak a mile wide and wouldn't admit he was wrong in filing the divorce papers. Amber might not believe in marriage for herself, but she'd made a living on happy endings. She didn't intend to let this one slip away.

"Great. Remember—Casey's at six. And make sure you wear something sexy."

Amber went back to work, though she couldn't stop thinking about Jake and what a mistake she could be making. As much as she pretended she could handle whatever he threw her way, her heart couldn't take another battering. That might be exactly what she would get if she kept seeing him. She would have to find a way to keep from getting too involved, at least on the emotional level. She didn't need him. Didn't need this kind of mess in her life. But what was she supposed to do? The way she saw it, she didn't have any other choice.

Every road in her life led back to Jake, and no matter how she tried to get away, she felt like she was running in circles.

 (R (R (R

A few minutes after six that night, Amber pushed open the heavy front door and walked into Casey's Bar. The scent of stale beer and peanuts, along with the cheers of the crowd of customers and the noises from the game playing on several TVs hung around the room, assaulted her senses. The door swung closed behind her with a bang, leaving her no choice but to make her way toward the bar.

The place reminded her of so many other businesses in town. Small, a little run-down, but always full of regulars who would squawk if anything changed. The people around here, in the mid-sized New England town, were such creatures of habit.

Amber glanced around the crowded room, recognizing more than a few faces. She finally caught sight of Jake sitting at the bar with a big, bulky man with a shock of blond hair. Steve. It had been a long time since she'd seen him. He hadn't changed a bit. She smiled. For once, Jake had actually come through for her, though she'd have to speak with him later about his choice of places to meet up. This place was a little too down home for her comfort.

She pushed her way through the throng of baseball fans and headed toward the men.

"Hello," a leering drunk slurred in her direction. He gave her a huge smile.

She ignored him and moved on. When she'd said to Jake to set up a meeting at a bar, she hadn't imagined he'd pick the seediest dive in town. What idiots men were sometimes. If she wanted something done right, she had to do it herself. Next time, she'd be the one to make the plans. She couldn't imagine Madison comfortable in a place like this, either.

Then again, maybe that was a good thing. It might push Steve to act more quickly in getting her out of there.

She reached the bar and put her hand on Jake's arm. "Hey."

"You made it. I'm glad you didn't change your mind." Jake smiled in her direction before turning to Steve. "You remember Amber Velez, don't you?"

Steve glanced at her and his eyes widened. His mouth opened, but no sound came out. Amber couldn't help the giggle that escaped. She'd seen people's reactions to her new self often enough around town to be used to it by now, but it still thrilled her a little bit each time. No one around here had ever imagined she'd grow up to be anything more than a plain, dowdy housewife. She'd proven them all wrong, and it made her smile even several weeks after she'd moved back.

"Hi, Steve."

"Hey, Amber." He blinked a few times, and finally a smile spread over his face. "Wow. You look different."

"Good different, or bad different?"

He gave her whole body a slow, meaningful perusal. When his gaze came back to hers, she caught a hint of blatant appreciation. "Definitely good."

"Thanks."

Jake stood. His arm came around her waist and he hauled her up against him, sealing his lips over hers for a fast, hard kiss that had her toes curling in her shoes. When he released her, he shot Steve a glare that clearly warned the other man not to do any more looking.

Amber pinched his side. "Relax, okay? Sit back down."

With a grumble, he settled back onto the stool he'd just vacated and motioned for Amber to take a seat next to him, on the opposite side of Jake from where Steve sat. She slid onto the seat, but kept her gaze on the door, waiting for Madison's arrival. She didn't have to wait long. Five minutes after Amber had arrived, Madison stepped through the door with the last man Amber had expected. Jake's younger brother, David.

Oh, crap.

Amber let out a breath. Why David, of all people? Couldn't Madison have found someone Steve didn't know? Well, they'd wanted to get a reaction out of Steve. That would certainly be happening now.

Madison and David chose a table in the center of the room. After they'd settled in, Madison glanced in Amber's direction and smiled. Amber smiled back, though she had a feeling things could get out of hand quickly, given the new turn the situation had taken. She leaned in to Jake.

"Hey. Did you see who just walked in?"

He squinted over his shoulder. A second later, his gaze swung to hers. "What the hell did you do?"

"I didn't do anything. That wasn't my idea."

"What's going on?" Steve asked. He looked around the room, and when his gaze fell on the table in the center, it hardened. "Who the hell is she here with?"

Jake shrugged, feigning interest in the bottle of beer the bartender had just set in front of him. "Who are you talking about?"

"Maddie. She's here with some young guy. She doesn't even like sports. What is she doing in a *sports* bar?" Steve coughed. "Christ, Jake. That's *David* she's with. What the hell is she doing?"

"Having a drink, apparently." Jake lifted the bottle to his lips and took a sip of the dark liquid.

Amber hung back and watched the exchange, proud of Jake for the way he managed to control himself, even though Madison had thrown a wrench into their plans by bringing his brother.

"That's bullshit." Steve's tone was harsh and his face had turned several shades of red.

"You're getting divorced, remember?"

Steve glanced at Jake and then at Madison and then at Jake again, and he shook his head. "I've got to get out of here. I can't watch this."

He stood, slapped a couple of bills on the bar, and rushed toward the door as if he couldn't escape fast enough. When he reached the door, he hesitated, turned around, and stomped over to the table where Madison sat with David. A few seconds later, David got up, his shoulders squared and his expression grim. Amber bit her lip to keep from smiling. Though they were too far away to hear what was being said, she had to give Madison credit. Maybe she *had* picked the right man for the job. David seemed to be going right along with the plan. *If* Madison had told him about the plan rather than led him to believe they were really on a date.

Watching the exchange between David and Steve, it struck Amber how much the Storm men looked alike. All tall and broad-shouldered like their father, they had the same brown hair and blue eyes. Even their features were similar. Looking at David, who couldn't be more than twenty-five, was like looking at Jake that summer they'd graduated high school. David was like a leaner, younger version of Jake and their middle brother, Brian. She smiled. It was a wonder none of them were married, that some woman had yet to snatch them up and lay claim to them.

"Are you okay?" Jake asked against her ear. He kissed her there and she shivered.

"I'm fine. I was just thinking how much you and David and Brian all look alike. No one could deny you're brothers."

He pulled back and rolled his eyes. "Women. You don't think this will escalate into a fist fight, do you?"

She shook her head. "David's too smart to let it come to that. Besides, I don't think Madison would let it happen, either. At least I hope not. Steve's a lot bigger than your brother."

Jake laughed. "David's strong. Don't underestimate him."

She didn't doubt it for a second. Growing up with a tough-as-nails police detective as a father, the Storm boys had learned early on how to defend themselves if the need arose.

The argument continued for a few more minutes, and Amber started to get worried. She was about to tell Jake to go over there and do something, but suddenly Madison stood, grabbed Steve's hand, and hauled him out the door. David ambled toward the bar and flopped onto the seat Steve had vacated not long before.

"Hey, guys." He smiled and shook his head. "That was pretty crazy, huh?"

"Yeah," Jake agreed. "I thought he was going to bash your pretty-boy face in."

"Wouldn't have happened." David glanced around Jake and smiled at Amber. "Hey, Amber. How are you?"

She returned his easy smile with one of her own. "Thanks for doing this tonight. I'm sure Madison appreciates it."

David shrugged. "I'm always happy to help out a couple of friends. Madison said they needed to go home, that they had a lot to talk about. Think they'll get back together?"

Lord, she hoped so. If anyone belonged together, it was the two of them. If Madison was willing to forgive Steve for his temporary insanity in asking for the divorce, Steve should at least meet her halfway and admit he was wrong. They would have a long way back to the place they'd been a few years ago, but Amber had seen enough couples in love to know what Steve and Madison had was the real thing. It was worth hanging onto, no matter what the sacrifice.

Jake leaned in again and kissed the side of her neck. "I'm ready to get out of here. What about you?"

A laugh bubbled up in her throat. "I've been ready since the second I got out of my car in the parking lot. Let's go."

"Are you leaving, too?" Jake asked David.

"Nah. I think I'm gonna stick around to see the rest of the game. You two kids have fun now. Don't do anything I wouldn't do."

Jake shook his head. "So that leaves pretty much anything open, huh?"

David only smiled.

A few minutes later, the tab paid, Jake led Amber out the door into the cool night air.

"That went well," she said.

"Yeah, I guess it did. I just hope Steve's not too upset."

"He should be upset. He's obviously a jerk if he'd walk out on his wife without any explanation."

"There are two sides to every story."

She stopped walking and glanced up at Jake. "I didn't say she was completely innocent."

"True. You didn't." He took her hand and gave it a reassuring squeeze. "So what should we do now that we're all alone?"

He waggled his eyebrows. She laughed. "Not what you're thinking."

"Who said I was thinking anything? Give me a little more credit than that, woman." His expression was wounded, but humor sparkled in his eyes.

She tugged her hand out of his and crossed her arms over her chest, her eyebrows raised. "Don't men think about sex every seven point nine seconds, or some absurd number like that?"

He laughed. "Yep. We do."

"So tell me you're not thinking about it right now."

"Just because I'm thinking about it doesn't mean anything. Though I have to admit, I've thought about it even more lately since you walked back into my life. It makes concentrating on other things, like work, a little difficult at times."

She understood the feeling. Since they'd started seeing each other again, even before she'd abandoned her plan, being with Jake had ruined her focus. If she hadn't been around him so much, her business would have been open already.

"You just want me for my body."

He shrugged. "Nah. Your mind is pretty interesting, too."

"Really?"

"Duh."

She wasn't one to succumb to warm and fuzzy feelings, but the sincerity in Jake's voice made her come pretty close. She wrapped her arms around herself and smiled. He admired her for her mind. He'd never really told her that before, though she'd always suspected. She'd known, years ago, he hadn't been attracted to her for her body.

"So what do you want to do?" she asked, grabbing his hand.

"It's warm outside. Why don't we go for a walk in the park?"

"This late?"

"Sure. Crime doesn't happen around here. And if anything does, don't worry. I'm here to protect you."

"Gee, thanks. That makes me feel so much better."

"It should. I'm a big, strong, tough guy."

"Yeah, sure you are." She laughed, but he was right. He was big and strong. Not tough, at least not usually, but driven. She'd seen that side of him when he'd stomped into her office that morning and threatened to swing her over his shoulder. His presence was a heck of a lot more commanding now than it had been growing up. He'd matured into an interesting, if not slightly domineering, man.

Damned if she didn't like this new facet of his personality.

They walked hand in hand down the street toward the park, enjoying the warmth of the Vermont spring night. They reached the entrance of the park. Jake held tight to her hand and gave it another squeeze, pulling her along the walkway that would lead them into the lush trees. There were a few other couples out enjoying the night. Soon he stopped their walking and leaned down to kiss her.

She let it go on for a few seconds before she stopped him. "What do you think you're doing?"

"If you don't know, I must not be doing it right."

"You're doing it right, believe me. But we aren't alone out here. There are a few other people right over there."

She pointed toward a group of college-aged kids loitering a hundred feet or so away. Jake took her hand, placed a kiss to the center of her palm, and smiled. His expression was so devious she swallowed hard.

"What are you planning?"

"You'll see."

He led her off the path, into a small cluster of trees, and pushed her up against the trunk of one. "See? No more people." He leaned down and kissed her again, slowly at first, but soon the kiss grew in intensity. He pressed his body to hers, his hands coming up to cup her breasts in his warm palms. When his thumbs flicked across her nipples, her panties dampened and she whimpered.

His lips left hers, trailing down the side of her neck until he reached the spot where it met her shoulder. He nipped there, and Amber let her head drop back against the rough bark of the tree trunk. A soft moan escaped her lips, though she was fighting to keep from crying out and alerting any passersby to their location.

Jake hiked her skirt above her hips, pushed her panties aside, and slipped a finger into her.

She gasped and put her hands on his shoulders. "Jake. This is a public place."

"Yeah, but we're all alone."

The heat in his eyes had her wanting to melt into a puddle at his feet. She swallowed past the lump in her throat and looked around. Just what she needed right before opening her business—to get arrested for public indecency. "I don't care if we're alone or not, this isn't—"

"Neither do I."

Before she could protest further, he leaned in and kissed her again. The wet warmth of his lips and tongue, combined with the feel of his body against her, made her want to scream in frustration. It was wrong to be outside, letting him touch her the way he was, but it didn't feel anything but right. And then he started to stroke his finger inside her and all protests evaporated from her mind. She no longer wanted to push him away. Instead, it made her want to draw him closer.

She wrapped her arms around his neck and held on, relishing in the delicious sensations coursing through her with every thrust of that finger, with every brush of his tongue against hers. Damn, the man knew how to turn her on.

Because he had a lot of practice.

Somehow the words didn't carry the warning they usually did. She felt herself sinking deeper and deeper into him until she knew there was no turning back. The man had probably been with every available woman in this county and all the surrounding ones too, but at the moment she didn't care. All she cared about was that he kept touching her, kept kissing her, and didn't stop.

He added a second finger inside her and she rocked her hips. His tongue dipped into her mouth, matching the rhythm of his fingers inside her. He nudged her legs apart with his knee and found her clit with his thumb. He pressed down against the nub of nerves, stroking his finger across it, and heat shot through her. It was the most incredible thing she'd ever experienced, and she'd been waiting for this moment with Jake all her life. For the first time, there was nothing between them. No secrets, no lies. It was just the two of them discovering what they could mean to each other.

The first stirrings of orgasm started low in her belly, and she didn't fight them. She went with them instead, holding onto Jake as the waves crashed over her, dragging her along. His mouth covered hers and he swallowed her cries.

When she floated back to earth, Jake pulled away and glanced down at her, heat in his eyes. His breath was coming almost as hard and fast as hers.

"You okay?"

She was more than okay. She was freakin' spectacular. He knew it, too. The look in his eyes told her that better than words ever could. If he let her go right now, she'd probably end up in a heap on the ground. "I'm fine."

"Just fine?"

"Okay, maybe a little better than fine."

He didn't respond, but gave her a smug smile. He stepped away, straightened out her panties and skirt, and took her hand, walking her back toward the bar parking lot where they'd left their cars.

"Where are we going now?"

Part of her was hoping he'd tell her he was taking her home. His bed or hers, it didn't matter at the moment. She just needed him inside her. He must need the same thing, given that she'd been the only one to get any satisfaction.

"We're supposed to be on a date, remember?" He glanced down at her and humor sparked in his eyes. "Where did you think we were going?"

Afraid he'd tease her, she didn't say a word.

"What's the matter, Amber?"

The tone in his voice told her he planned to tease her anyway. She narrowed her eyes. "Not a thing."

"You sure?"

"I'm not the one who didn't come, in case you've forgotten. I'm not the one with the problem right now."

His soft groan made her laugh. "I haven't forgotten, but it isn't important. We can worry about that later. I told you I wanted to see you tonight, and I meant it. I don't want to jump into bed. I want to spend a little time with you first."

His tone warned her he had something specific in mind. She glanced up at him and shook her head. What wasn't he telling her? "What do you have planned?"

"Something." He winked. "You'll see."

ೞ ೞ ೞ

Jake set the tray down on the worn picnic table and settled onto the bench across from Amber. The lights from the take-out windows of the diner played across her eyes, and he couldn't help but be reminded of the last time they'd come here.

It had been the summer after graduation, and they'd come down to get something to eat after a long night of talking. Discussing their respective futures and where they wanted to end up when they finished college. It had been just before midnight, and the diner that had been a favorite hangout of the kids in town was the only thing open that late.

He'd never come here with Amber when it had been busy, and he hated himself for that now. So what if she wasn't beautiful then? Her friendship should have been all that mattered. He should have been strong enough to not worry about what anyone else thought, but back then he'd been too worried about popularity and hanging out with the right crowd—at least the crowd he'd thought at the time was the right one. Now he realized how stupid and selfish his actions were, but it was too late to take them back.

He let out a soft curse before picking up a burger and peeling back the wrapper.

"Why did you want to come here?" Amber asked. She had yet to touch any of the food. Instead she sat there, hands folded in front of her and her questioning gaze focused on him.

"It has good memories for me." He remembered countless after-dark study sessions and talks they had sitting at one of the quiet picnic tables closer to the back, under the flickering lights that lined the property. "I didn't even think that you might not eat this kind of food anymore. All the calories. I guess I should have realized."

She raised an eyebrow.

"I didn't mean it like that. Just that you're skinny now and before you were…" *Shit.* He shook his head and scrubbed his hand down his face. Every word was digging him in deeper and deeper. Soon there would be no way out. The best thing to do would be to shut up before he went too far, but for some reason he couldn't keep his mouth closed. "You're gorgeous now. Not that you weren't back then, but now you're just…and…Christ. Will you stop me already?"

Her husky laugh filled the air around them and tickled his senses. "Relax. I know what you mean, even if you do have a strange way of saying it. I didn't watch what I ate then. I do now, but I can make an exception once in a while. What would life be without a little fun, right?"

As if to prove her point, she snagged a golden French fry from the box and popped it into her mouth. She chewed slowly, her eyes half closed, and let out a soft sigh when she finished. "Man. I'd forgotten how good greasy piles of fat taste."

He had to laugh at her comment. She was so cute tonight he couldn't help but want to pull her close and kiss her. He would kiss her, too, just not yet. Once they finished eating and he took her home, there would be plenty of time for kissing. And more. She wanted him as much as he wanted her. He could see it in her eyes. In her smile. Even in the way she carried herself, as if she knew she was driving him out of his friggin' mind, and she was enjoying every second of it.

He'd been worried earlier, when he'd all but dragged her out of her office. There had been a horrible few minutes where he'd thought she'd tell him to leave her alone. That she'd only wanted revenge, and now that she'd had it, she was finished with him. He was a lucky bastard that she'd given him a second chance. He wanted to be upset with her for what she'd done, and he had been at first, but he couldn't quite manage the emotion anymore. What he'd done to her had been worse than anything she could ever do, no matter how long she stayed with him.

"You look good, you know." She had to know. The woman had a mirror or two in her apartment, but he also felt like he had to tell her. He hadn't been nice in the past few minutes, and before, years ago, he'd never once told her she was pretty. She deserved to hear it at least a hundred times a day.

"And you're surprised?"

"I just expected you to grow up different, you know?"

"How so?"

"I figured you'd be a marine biologist or a doctor or something." He was the one who hadn't been serious about school, at least not like Amber had been, and he'd ended up getting into Harvard Law. He'd made good grades in high school, but had thought off and on about skipping college and traveling around the world for a year or two. Luckily, he'd come to his senses. Law had always interested him.

"I thought about it, but four years at NYU was enough. More than enough. By the time I finished my freshman year, I'd changed so much that I couldn't stand the thought of extended schooling. I'd been so busy being serious that I hadn't had much in the way of teenage years, so I'd had it. I ended up majoring in business and the wedding planner thing sort of just happened."

She smiled and snagged another fry. This time she didn't just pop it into her mouth. She slid it in slowly, in a way that had him swallowing hard and imagining those full lips on his body instead. He shifted on the bench.

"So why law?" she asked him when she finished chewing. "I thought you'd become a pro baseball player or something."

"I'd thought about it, but in the end decided that might not get me where I needed to go in life. I thought about becoming a police officer or detective like my dad, but I'd always been interested in law and I decided to go for it and make a career out of it."

"Do you do okay around here? I mean, I can't see there being that much divorce here."

"There's more than you think. Marriage is sort of a pastime around here, in the middle of practically nowhere. Just look at Amanda. She's had three divorces." He shrugged. "I do other types of work, too, family stuff and the occasional defense when someone hits something with their car, but it can be quiet sometimes."

He made enough to live comfortably, especially since it was just him. He had a nice, if not a little small, house, a new car, and no problems paying the bills and getting what he needed. He'd even splurged on his wide-screen TV and the accompanying surround-sound system, but he wouldn't consider himself rich. Comfortable would be a better description.

"It must be interesting work."

"It can be, but I have to say, my mother—and yours—try to get all the latest gossip out of me. They don't understand the whole attorney-client privilege thing. Dodging them has become interesting over the past few years."

She laughed and reached for a hamburger, unwrapping a corner of the wrapper and taking a bite. They ate in silence for a little while before Amber crumpled her wrapper and pushed it to the side. "I'm full."

"Are you kidding me? You hardly ate anything."

"I ate enough. A burger and a few fries is what fills me up. I'm not a giant like you. I don't need the same amount of calories."

He laughed. "Okay, I guess that's true. I just don't want you to feel like you can't eat around me. Believe me, seeing a woman eat doesn't turn me off."

"If I ate whatever I wanted, whenever I wanted, I'd be as big as a house again. I'm not willing to take that route. I like how I look now, but I have to be careful, especially right now since I've been too busy to get to the gym."

"Is that all you're worried about? If it's a workout you want, I can give you one."

Amber licked her lips. A slow, sexy smile spread over her face. "Oh, yeah?"

"Absolutely."

"Then what are you waiting for?"

"I have no idea."

There had been something, but the second he'd caught the heat in her eyes, his reasons for waiting had slipped his mind. Now, with her looking at him like she wanted to eat him alive, he couldn't manage to string together a single coherent thought. He crumpled his own food wrappers, dropped them on the tray, and stood to walk the tray over to the garbage can a few dozen feet away.

When he walked back to the table, Amber had stood and was smoothing her skirt down her thighs. He swallowed hard, thinking about how that same short skirt had been up around her waist earlier in the park. It was all he could do not to pull her behind the shed at the back of the property, shove that skirt back up, and sink himself into her.

She caught him looking and beckoned him with her finger. "Are we getting out of here yet?"

He nodded, grabbing her hand and pulling her toward his car. "Sure are. We're going back to your place for the night."

"What about my car? It's still at Casey's."

Like he had time to worry about that now. "We'll get it sometime tomorrow. For now, I have other plans for you."

Chapter Nine

Amber poured coffee into her mug, added milk and sugar, and took it to the couch for her morning ritual of watching the news while she drank her much-needed dose of heavenly caffeine. She'd taken a shower and gotten ready to head down to the office, and Jake hadn't even gotten out of bed yet. She laughed softly to herself. The man could sleep through anything.

Last night had been amazing. Even better than the time before. Probably because she'd somehow managed to forget all the pain of the past and just let herself be free to be with Jake and care about him. Finally, *finally*, she was able to let it all go and come to terms with the fact she still had feelings for him. They weren't the same people they'd been all those years ago. They'd changed, and their lives and dreams and goals had changed with them.

She took another sip of her coffee and relaxed against the couch cushions, her gaze traveling around the small space inside her apartment. It wasn't where she wanted to be forever, but it worked for right now. Later on, she'd have to look for a bigger place—once she could afford it, she might even consider buying a house. The past few days, she'd started thinking about settling down. She'd never had the interest before, but now she couldn't get the idea out of her mind.

She let her head drop back against the cushion and groaned. This was about Jake. Of course. It had to be. As much as she'd tried to convince herself otherwise, she wasn't over the guy. She'd come back home thinking about raking him over the coals, rubbing him raw and then walking away, and now all she could think about was two-story houses, white picket fences, and—shudder—minivans.

Well, hell. Any more complications that feel like raining down on me today?

She should have known better than to ask. A knock sounded on the door and she got up to answer it, wondering who would be at her door at just after seven on a Saturday morning. Her mother or Adele, probably, given the fact that they seemed to think eight a.m. was a perfectly reasonable time to pay a visit. It had happened too many times over the past few weeks, and she really needed to speak to them about that.

After a quick stop in the kitchen area to set down her mug, she stretched her arms over her head and walked to the door. She glanced out the peephole and found the one person she really didn't want to see. Zack. *Crap.*

How was she supposed to handle this? She'd told him it was over when she'd given him back his ring and moved away, but he'd promised he wasn't ready to let her go. She hadn't really expected him to follow her, but by now, she should have learned to expect the unexpected.

She glanced over her shoulder toward the bedroom, where Jake lay still sleeping, before she opened the door.

Zack didn't say a word, and didn't give her a chance to speak, either. Instead, he pulled her in for a huge, tight hug. It seemed to last forever. By the time he let her go, she could barely breathe.

"God, I've missed you," he said, a big smile on his face. "It's been way too long."

She blinked. It had been a matter of weeks, not even a month yet, since she'd seen him last. "What are you doing here?"

"I know you said it was over, but I wanted to see you. Had to. I couldn't stay away any longer."

"You could have called." If he had, she would have told him not to bother coming. She crossed her arms over her chest. "You really shouldn't be here, Zack."

"I know. You told me it was done between us, and I tried to accept that, but in the end I couldn't. I need you back, Amber. I'm lost without you."

Yeah, because she was the one who'd organized his filing cabinets. He probably couldn't find anything on his own since she'd put things away. He didn't need her the way he thought he did. The way his family had convinced him he did. His mother had pushed them together right from the start, and Zack had gone along with it. Amber didn't believe for one second that Lorna Morales hadn't sent her son here. This didn't seem like the type of thing Zack would do on his own.

"Don't start. I said it was over, and I meant it. I can't marry you."

"Just give me one more chance to prove to you that this can work. We're good for each other. A partnership between us would be perfect."

Partnership? That sounded like something another member of his family would say. Namely his father, who wanted grandchildren. Male ones to carry on the Morales name and take over the lucrative manufacturing business that had been in their family for generations.

Amber had no interest in anything they could offer her. If she ever got married, and that was a *big* if, she would do it for no other reason but love. Money and social status would have no bearing on her decision. She did love Zack, but only as a friend. Not the way she'd have to love a man in order to make a lifetime commitment to him.

"How can you even be here right now? What about work?" Work had always been important to him. He had to carry on the family business.

"I took a week's vacation. I'm staying at the cheesy little hotel down the street since there really isn't anything else around. Can I come in so we can talk or are you going to keep me standing out here all morning?"

Not wanting to wake up her few neighbors, she opened the door wider and stepped back. "Fine, come inside, but just for a few minutes."

He walked into the apartment and she shut the door behind him, her teeth snagging and chewing on her lower lip. This was *so* not good. Jake in the bedroom, Zack in the main living space, and Amber stuck in the middle of a place she really had no desire to be. It was Jake she wanted, but she had a feeling this could turn ugly very easily. Zack wasn't one to let go of something once he'd decided he wanted it, even if he wanted it for all the wrong reasons.

"So, how have you been?" he asked, and she nearly winced. Same old Zack, dressed in khakis and a button-down shirt even on vacation. Not a single dark hair was out of place.

"Busy. I have no time for a social life since I'm trying to set up my own business." Between setting up the business, her family, and Jake, she hadn't had a free second to herself in too long. This was the first moment she'd been able to steal, and Zack had interrupted.

"I know. It must be tough."

What the hell did he know about it? He'd always gotten everything handed to him. The guy wouldn't even need to work if he didn't want to.

She pushed the negative thoughts away. It wasn't Zack she was upset with. It was the situation. Things were such a mess right now and could only get worse from here. She took a deep breath and swiped a hand through her hair. With any luck, Jake would sleep right through the visit and she could put off dealing with this for all that much longer.

"It hasn't been too bad, just tiring. How have you been?"

"Missing you."

Laying it on a little thick, aren't we? Just when she'd convinced herself he wasn't all that bad, he had to come in with something like that. "I would think your family would want you to find someone a little more suitable for you. I don't come from money, and I don't have the breeding she seems to favor."

"My mother loves you. She's always wanted me to settle down with a nice Latina girl."

So that was what it all came down to. She shook her head. "I'm only half. My father is Venezuelan. My mother's Italian."

"I know. That's not what I meant, Amber, and you know it."

She shook her head. She wasn't going to be anyone's token wife, no matter how much he kept telling her he cared about her.

"Look, Zack, you really shouldn't be here. I'm not interested in getting back together, so if that's what you've come to town for, you're wasting your time."

His expression fell for a second, but soon his gaze filled with the typical steely resolve she'd always seen there. He reached for her and she ducked away.

"I don't think I am wasting my time. Not at all."

"How do you figure?"

"We've always had a good relationship. You wouldn't have agreed to marry me in the first place if you didn't care. So you got a little scared. So what? I can show you that we can be together. Just give me a second chance."

Zack really was so different from Jake that it almost made her laugh. Where Zack looked like he was about ready to drop at her feet and beg, Jake would have slung her over his shoulder, dragged her someplace quiet, and not let her go until she admitted he was right. Even if he wasn't. Just the thought of Jake slinging her over his shoulder again made her hot everywhere.

She shook off the out-of-place feeling and tried to force herself back to the matter at hand. Hearing Zack out and getting rid of him before Jake woke up took top priority. Zack was a huge complication she had no use for in the new life she was trying to build for herself.

"Do I have a choice in the matter, or have you already made up your mind?"

"Of course. You always have a choice." He smiled. "But I'm not going away until I've had a chance to convince you. I'm here to stay, Amber, until you're ready to come back home with me."

A cough from the other side of the room drew both of their attention. Amber swung her gaze to the kitchen door, where Jake stood in nothing but a pair of jeans, a sleepy expression on his face.

"Am I missing something important here?" he asked, his tone laced with aggravation.

Amber glanced at Zack before returning her attention to Jake. "No. Why don't you go back to bed and get a little more sleep? I'll join you in a few minutes."

"Who the hell is that?" Zack asked, his irritated gaze moving between Amber and Jake. He finally fixed Amber with a hard glare. "All this time I've been standing here, pouring my heart out to you, and you aren't even alone. Amazing, how fast you can dump me and move on to someone new. Why didn't you tell me you had company?"

The way he said the last word made her wince. She'd never seen Zack angry before, but she had a feeling she was about to. "Because it isn't really any of your business. You didn't give me a chance to say anything, anyway. You just barged in here and started in telling me you were here and had no plans to leave. I don't need this from you right now. I never asked for you to come here, Zack. You did that all on your own."

Jake leaned against the doorframe and cleared his throat, obviously not wanting to be forgotten. "Who's your friend, Amber?"

"Don't start, Jake."

"What? I'm just curious." His hard expression was anything but. His shoulders were stiff and a muscle ticked in his jaw. "Aren't you going to introduce me?"

Sure. Why the hell not. It couldn't get any more uncomfortable than it already was. "This is Zack. Zack, this is Jake."

Nothing like the past and the present mingling into one big, huge uncomfortable ball that settled in the bottom of her stomach like lead.

Zack was the first to speak. "Jake? That's the guy you left me for? How could you be back with *him* after what he did to you?"

He took a step toward Jake, his hands clenching into fists, and Amber tugged on his sleeve to get him to stop. "Knock it off, Zack. I don't see how that's any of your business. So what if I am? People change. They *grow up*."

"Eighteen is hardly a kid."

Jake walked over to the coffee maker and poured himself a cup of coffee. He added a little milk from the carton in the fridge and settled onto one of the barstools at the counter. Amber rolled her eyes. Obviously he wasn't going anywhere. Zack's expression told her he was here to stay, too.

What had she ever done to deserve this?

There was that little matter of deceiving Jake to prove a point she should have gotten over a long time ago, but in the grand scheme of things, how big was that really?

Pretty damned huge, apparently.

Jake said nothing, but he kept shooting glares at Zack. Zack did the same, and it didn't take Amber long to get sick of dealing with all the stupid male posturing. She took the mug from Jake's hands, ignoring his surprised glare, and dumped the coffee down the drain. The mug hit the sideboard with a thump and she turned to face them, hands on her hips.

"You're both unbelievable. Neither one of you own me. I want you both out. *Now.* I have a very busy day planned and I don't have time for a couple of jerks on ego trips."

Jake narrowed his eyes. Without a word, he walked into the bedroom and slammed the door.

"Wow. He's got a temper." Zack let out a low whistle. "Better watch out for him. I'd hate to see what he's like when he really gets angry."

Of all the stupid, transparent things to say. "He wouldn't be upset if you hadn't shown up here and tried to lay claim to something that doesn't belong to you."

Zack raised his eyebrows. His smile fell and he spread his arms out in front of him, palms up. "Are you saying that you belong to him?

Inside, Amber seethed. She balled her hands into fists, but soon the urge to hit Zack got to be too strong and she clasped her hands in front of her to keep from following through. "I'm saying that I don't *belong* to anyone. Neither of you has the right to act like this."

A few seconds later, Jake came out of the bedroom, fully dressed. He walked over to Amber, tugged her right up against him, and gave her a hot kiss that had her knees buckling. His tongue stroked into her mouth once, twice, before he broke away and gave her a heated smile. "Are you working today?"

Unable to speak, she nodded.

"I'll call you tonight, then. Maybe we can do dinner or something."

Without even a glance at Zack, he walked out the door. Amber watched him go, her whole body still tingling from the kiss. She forgot Zack was even in the room until he spoke.

"Oh, I get it now."

"Get what?" she asked without looking at him.

"What you see in him. It's all about the sex, isn't it?"

"No. That's only part of it."

"Is that why you left me? Because we never set the sheets on fire?"

She glanced at him out of the corner of her eye and shook her head. "It's not like that. We were good together. But with Jake, it's different."

"Whatever he does for you, I could do it, too."

The determination in Zack's tone made her wince. How could she explain something to him that she didn't fully understand herself? "No. I don't think you can. It's not something he consciously does. It's just something that's there between us. You can't turn it on and off."

"Wanna bet?"

"Zack, please don't do this. Can't you just let me be happy?"

He walked to the door and yanked it open, looking over his shoulder at her. "I've said it a hundred times, and I'll say it a hundred more, if that's what it takes. I'm not ready to let you go."

Without giving her a chance to respond, he stormed out and slammed the door behind him.

Chapter Ten

The next Wednesday night, Jake sat at Casey's, waiting for Steve. He swirled his drink around in the glass. Hard liquor this time, rather than the usual bottle of beer. It had been a long few days at work, made longer by the fact that though he'd spoken to Amber, she'd been too busy to see him. Getting her office ready to open was her excuse and he had to believe it, but it still smarted that she wouldn't make time to meet him for lunch. Especially with her ex-fiancé in town.

Funny, but she'd failed to mention the fact that the ex—Zack—was rich. And gorgeous, according to Amanda, who'd run into him a few days earlier. He wanted her back, too. Amber would be stupid to choose Jake when she had a man all but begging to marry her. A man who could give her everything she'd ever want and need. Why settle for a small town lawyer when she could have everything?

Cut the shit, a voice in his head warned. *You're getting too attached. It's only been a few weeks.*

He took another gulp of the vodka. That was the truth. It had only been a few days since he'd seen her. He wouldn't be worrying about it, if her ex-fiancé hadn't suddenly shown up. The man was perfect as far as Jake could tell, and obviously had no problems flaunting his money, with the way he drove that hundred-thousand dollar car around town and dressed like he'd just stepped out of some ridiculous fashion magazine.

Jake did well, but he didn't make the kind of money that would buy him a car like the one Zack drove. According to Amber, Zack had never hurt her the way Jake had. The only thing he'd ever done was love her. Jake wouldn't blame her if she did want to go back to the guy—though he didn't have to like it.

He downed the rest of the vodka in one gulp and signaled the bartender for another. Might as well get drunk tonight, since he had nothing better to do. At least then he might not feel sorry for himself.

He hadn't wanted to get involved with Amber. He really hadn't. But every time he saw her, he sank deeper and deeper into a place he couldn't find a way out of. Now he was stuck. Miserable. What the hell was he supposed to do about it?

The bartender set a full glass on the bar in front of Jake and walked away without a word. Jake lifted it to his lips to take a sip. It was his third, and really needed to be his last. If Steve didn't get here soon, he might have to cut himself off and grab a cab back to his house.

Halfway through the drink, Steve showed up and settled onto the stool next to Jake. The game was going on, and they used to hang out at Steve's or Jake's house to watch it along with Brian and sometimes David, but with Steve's impending divorce, it seemed more suited to meet on neutral ground.

"You're a mess tonight," Steve commented after he ordered a beer. "What's up with the vodka? Women troubles?"

He didn't know the half of it. Jake himself had yet to figure it all out. "Something like that."

"Wanna talk about it?"

Talk? What the fuck good would talking do, anyway? It would only get him more pissed off, and that was a place he didn't really want to be.

This was what he got for getting involved with Amber again. He should have known better. *Had* known better, right from the start. Instead of walking away like his mind had urged him to, he'd followed his body's direction and ended up getting his heart involved. It sucked, and he couldn't deal with this any longer. It was eating him up inside, wondering when she was going to leave him and head back to New York with Zack. She *would* leave, too. She'd be stupid not to, and Amber was anything but stupid.

"No, I don't want to talk about it." Jake polished off the rest of the glass and slammed it down on the bar.

"You gonna give me your keys?" Steve asked. His tone was quiet, but Jake caught a hint of worry there. He let out a bitter laugh.

"This isn't like you," Steve continued. "You're worrying me."

Not wanting to argue, Jake took them out of his pocket and slid them across the bar to Steve. "Here."

"I thought I was the one who was supposed to be a mess over a woman. What's brought this about?"

"Amber. Her *ex* is in town. Her rich, snotty asshole of an ex who swears he's going to get her back. He wants to marry her."

"And you think she's going to go back to him?"

He didn't think it, he knew it. He snorted. "What the hell do I care? I don't want to get married."

"You don't have to want to get married to fall in love."

Jake glanced at Steve out of the corner of his eye. He let out a breath. "I don't want that, either. Never have. It's too complicated."

"Sometimes you don't want it, but it sneaks up on you anyway. It pounces, and by the time you notice, it's too fucking late."

"Is that what happened with you and Madison?"

Steve was silent for a long time. When he finally answered, a haunted look passed across his eyes. "Yeah. I wasn't ready for it."

"You were married for seven years. It took you that long to notice?"

"Yeah. No." He shook his head. "I don't know. The only thing I do know is that I love her."

Jake had known that, but still Steve's confession shocked him. Steve had spent the past month trying to convince Jake that his love for Madison had faded away. Jake had known better, and now it seemed Steve was finally figuring that out. "Still do?"

"Yeah. I think I might have made a mistake."

"No shit." *About freakin' time, too.*

He glared at Jake. "What's that supposed to mean?"

"I *know* you still love her. She loves you, too. Why do you think she came in here with David the other night?"

"Why?"

"To make you jealous, you idiot. She wants you back, though with the way you've been acting, I have no clue why."

Steve sighed. He drank half his bottle of beer before he answered. "You set me up."

"Someone had to. It was Amber's idea, actually."

"Why did you go along with it?"

"Because you and Madison belong together. And because you're both my friends, and I'm sick of being pulled in two different directions. I don't want to choose sides. It's not fair for either of you to ask me to."

Steve seemed to think about Jake's words for a few minutes. "I'm sorry. I didn't see it that way."

"No big deal." At the moment, he had his own problems to deal with. Problems that didn't seem to have a happy solution.

"Think she'll take me back?" Steve asked, his tone hopeful.

"Talk to her and find out. I think she probably would. She wouldn't have tried to make you jealous if she didn't care." Jake paused. "What happened the other night after you two left here, anyway?"

Steve shrugged. "Nothing much. We argued. Then she got pissed and walked away. I wanted to go home with her, but I fucked everything up by asking for the divorce, so I was afraid to ask. Afraid she'd tell me to go to hell. That she didn't want me home again. Ever."

How stupid could a guy get? Hadn't Steve noticed Madison still loved him? Hadn't he bothered asking her feelings before he filed the divorce papers?

"Are you ready to act like a married man again?"

"I never stopped. I thought I wanted one thing, but it turns out the only thing I wanted was Madison. I just hope I haven't screwed that up too bad."

"You probably have, but Madison is a great woman. I'm sure she understands that men do stupid things. The only thing you can do is talk to her."

"I'm going to. I called her a little while ago. She wants to meet for coffee later so we can talk." He shook his head. "Wish me luck. I think I'm going to need it. I'll be right back. I have a phone call I have to make."

Jake slumped against the bar. Things looked promising for Steve and Madison. He wished he could say the same for himself. It was his own damned fault he'd fallen into this mess. As soon as he'd figured out Amber was out for revenge, he should have walked away without looking back. He'd been too stupid to follow his common sense, and look where it had gotten him. At a bar, drinking his troubles away.

Steve came back ten minutes later and slid onto the barstool. "I'm headed out to meet Maddie now. You going to be okay?"

Jake shrugged. "Are you going to give me my keys back?"

"You're not going to drive."

"Hell no, but if I take a cab home, I need to be able to get into my house. My house key's on that ring, too."

"I think that's where I come in." Amber stepped around Steve and took the keys he handed her. "Ready to go, Jake?"

He gaped at her in surprise for a few seconds before he recovered the power of speech. What the hell was she doing here? And how had she known he'd need a ride home? Steve. Jake muttered a curse. Steve's phone call had been to Amber.

"I'd rather take a cab. I don't need your help."

"Actually, I think you do. Besides, we really should talk, don't you think?"

"Do I look like I'm in any state to talk right now?"

She just shrugged. "I have plenty of time to wait. Come on, tough guy. Let's get out of here."

ଔ ଔ ଔ

Amber pulled her car up in front of Jake's house and switched off the engine. She turned to face him and shook her head. "I'll take you down to the bar in the morning to pick up your car."

A spark of something akin to hope took root inside him. "Does that mean you're staying tonight?"

"If you want me to."

Of course he wanted her to. He'd never wanted anything more. But she didn't look like she wanted to be anywhere near him right now.

"What about Zack?"

She sighed, staring out the windshield for a long time. When she finally answered, her voice was soft. "He's still in town, but I think you know that."

Jake fumed inside. He clenched his hands into fists. So she was still seeing the guy. "You know what, don't bother coming inside. I can make it up the damned front steps by myself."

He got out of the car and slammed the door behind him. He was halfway up the walk before he realized she'd followed.

She grabbed his arm. "Where are you going?"

"What the hell does it matter? You don't need me. Your fiancé wants you back."

"So what? Maybe I don't want him."

"Maybe, or you definitely don't?"

"Jake, don't start. This isn't really the time or the place for an argument."

He narrowed his eyes. She wouldn't deny it, and he wasn't going to beg for her to. He stalked up the walkway toward the front steps, reaching the front door in a few seconds. It wasn't until he'd gotten there that he realized she still had his keys.

"Looking for something?" she asked, as if reading his mind again. Her footsteps sounded on the wooden porch behind him.

He spun and held his hand out. "Yeah. I need my keys so I can get inside."

Instead of putting them in his hand, she stared at him for a long time, her expression filled with pain and regret. Finally, she stepped forward and wrapped her arms around his waist, resting her cheek on his chest. Unable to hold himself stiff, Jake put his arms around her.

"Please stay tonight, Amber. Please tell me you want to be here with me, right now. I don't care what'll happen later, tomorrow when you wake up and decide you're sick of me. I just want tonight with you."

She pulled back enough to look up at him. Tears shone in her eyes, and he couldn't help muttering a curse. He'd put those tears there. Again.

"I want to be here. I wouldn't have come to get you if I didn't."

That was all he needed to hear. He leaned down and crushed her lips with his.

Chapter Eleven

Amber sank into the kiss, even though she knew it was wrong. He'd had a few drinks—not a lot but enough that she questioned his state of mind. She should walk away, but right now she couldn't. She just wanted to be with him, even if it was the wrong decision to make.

Jake broke the kiss and took a step back, his hand raised and his palm up. "Give me the keys."

She dug in her purse, shaking fingers fumbling until she was able to pull the ring out and drop it into his hand. "Here."

"Thanks."

He didn't say another word as he unlocked the door, held her hand and led her inside. Once the door was shut and locked behind them, he took her purse from her and dropped it onto the small, round table by the door.

"Your house is really nice," she said, her gaze scanning the area around them.

"Yeah. I'll show you around later. Come here." He reached for her hand and pulled her toward the stairs.

"Where are we going?"

"To bed."

He said the words as if she should have been expecting them, and she had, but at the same time she'd been hoping for some time to talk with him, too. They hadn't been on the best of terms lately, and it had been eating away at her little by little. She'd missed him.

"Are you sure this is what you want?" she asked, trying to stall for time.

"I would have told you to go home if it wasn't."

He started walking up the stairs, his grip tight on her hand, and she had no choice but to follow. Once they reached his bedroom—a large, white room dominated by a king-sized bed—Amber pulled out of his grasp. She did want him. She wouldn't deny it, but she'd been hoping for more. Instead it felt like they were stuck in a cycle of misunderstandings, and as far as she could see, there was no hope of getting out anytime soon.

"Are you still upset with me?" she asked.

"No."

"Are you sure?"

He let out a heavy breath and turned to face her. He scrubbed a hand down his face. "I'm not upset with you. I don't know what I am. It's complicated, and I can't deal with anything complicated right now. But this, here between us, is simple. I want you. It doesn't get any more basic than that."

He stepped toward her and flicked the strap of her tank top off her shoulder before leaning down and kissing the spot the strap had just been. She sucked in a breath, her body swaying toward him. It suddenly felt like forever since he'd touched her.

His lips trailed along her skin until they reached hers, and he pulled her in for a kiss. The buildup was slow this time as he tasted her, as if trying to learn and memorize her. Her breath hitched at his tenderness—but the tenderness didn't last long. Soon his fingers were tearing at her clothes, yanking her top over her head, working the button at the waistband of her pants. Once he had them unzipped, he patted her hip. "Lose these."

"Jake, I—"

"We'll talk later, Amber. I promise."

The heat in his eyes made her gulp. He was a man whose control hung by a thread, and just the thought of him losing it sent a shock of heat spiraling through her body. With shaking fingers she complied, pushing her pants down and stepping out of them, at the same time toeing off her shoes. Her bra and panties followed, leaving her standing open and naked before him.

His gaze traveled down the length of her before coming back up and snagging hers. The intensity she found there made her heart beat a little faster. Within seconds he'd stripped out of his own clothes and strode toward her, all powerful, sexy man. A shiver ran from her head to her toes.

When he reached her, he took her hand and led her to the bed. Once there, he moved behind her, pressing his front to her back. He cupped her breasts in his palms and kneaded the globes of flesh until she squirmed.

"Jake, please."

"What's wrong?" His words were nothing more than a hot whisper against her ear.

"I don't want to wait tonight."

"I thought you wanted to wait. Thought you wanted to talk."

"Not anymore."

She felt his smile on the side of her neck. After a second, he released her and backed up. "Fine. We won't wait tonight, then. Get on the bed. On your hands and knees."

Her breath caught in her throat and she trembled. "What?"

"I want to take you from behind tonight. I have to warn you, though, I'm not really in the mood to be gentle."

"I don't have a problem with that." In fact, it made a quiver rush through her inner muscles. She did as he asked, settling in on the mattress. Her body thrummed with a delicious, nervous energy that had her barely able to hold still. "Jake?"

"Huh?" He walked to the night stand and opened the drawer. The sound of foil tearing filled the air, and a few seconds later, he came back to the bed and knelt behind her.

Still, he didn't touch her, though, and she pressed back, trying to put her body in contact with his. His hands came down on her ass and he massaged her cheeks in his palms. She let out a small whimper, suddenly more than ready for him. Her sex had been wet since they'd kissed outside on his front porch, and every word, every touch since then had only served to drive her higher. She didn't need preliminaries tonight, and something told her he understood.

The tip of his cock prodded her entrance just before he pushed inside. He entered her slowly at first, but once he'd seated himself fully he drew back and thrust in again, hard enough to pitch her forward on the mattress. When she didn't protest, he did it again, and she just about came out of her skin. The primal act thrilled her like nothing had before. Her inner muscles contracted around him. Her nipples ached and a moan escaped her lips.

He wound her hair around his hand, holding her in place while he hammered into her. Her breathing came hard and fast—she barely had a chance to catch a breath before she found herself sucking in another. His thumb pressed between her legs and found her clit. He swirled his thumb over the tight bud as his thrusts grew harder, faster, and she felt the orgasm building inside her. She tried to hang on as long as she could, wanting to come with him, but in the end she couldn't hold back. Heat and light exploded in her body, dragging her along as wave after wave of intense pleasure rocketed through her.

Jake released her hair and her elbows buckled, her upper body dropping to the mattress. His hands came to her hips and he tugged her hard against him, his body stiffening behind her as he came. Once he released her and pulled out, they both collapsed to the mattress in a tangle of sweaty limbs. It seemed like an eternity that they lay there, basking in the mutual afterglow. Amber's whole body tingled and a smile crept up her face. Even a quickie with Jake was incredible. He could turn her on with just a look.

Slowly, reality began to sink in and she moved away. Things were still so uncertain between them, and it had been a mistake to jump into bed with him without getting things settled first.

"Jake?" she asked in a whisper.

"Don't talk right now. I don't want to deal with anything. Let's just enjoy the moment and not ruin it, okay?"

His words, along with his aggravated tone, made her stiffen. She sat up and moved toward the top of the bed, resting her back against the headboard and pulling her knees up to her chest. Had tonight meant anything to him at all? She'd hoped they would be able to work out their problems, but it seemed he wasn't interested. Coming inside with him tonight had been a huge error in judgment.

"No. It's not okay. The last time we spoke, things weren't left well between us. We need to work through that, or it's always going to be there."

"Funny, but you never really wanted to work through anything before." He rolled onto his side and propped his head up with his hand, his elbow bent. "Why now, of all times, are you suddenly feeling the need to hash out everything you think is wrong between us? Does any of this really matter to you? We both know you're just going to go running back to your rich fiancé in the end."

Amber faced Jake across the bed. She was tired, worn out, and sick of fighting what she really wanted and what she didn't want at all. She was being pulled in too many directions and it felt like she might snap at any second. Between Jake and Zack and feelings she wanted no part of, she could no longer make sense of her own mind, let alone her life.

She swallowed hard at the searching look in Jake's eyes. He wanted something from her, though he hadn't yet asked. She was glad for that, because it was something she wasn't really ready to give. Maybe she never would be. Some things just weren't destined to happen, no matter how much a person might want them to.

"I'm sorry. I shouldn't have said that. I think we've both been under a lot of stress lately. Are you okay?" Jake asked. The hesitancy in his tone made her stomach ache. She didn't want to hurt him, but what choice did she have? With a man like Jake, there was no guarantee of forever. It was either hurt or be hurt, and she'd rather be on the other end of the spectrum this time.

"Yeah. I'm fine. Why?"

"You look like you want to leave."

"It isn't that. I just don't know where we're supposed to go from here. Are you sure this is what you even wanted tonight? You're drunk."

Anger glazed his eyes and he pressed his lips together so tightly they turned white at the corners. He stared at her for what felt like an eternity before he spoke.

"That's complete bullshit. I had three drinks. I know enough not to drive home after that. That's the only reason Steve had my keys. The *only* reason. I might have a buzz, but I'm not *drunk*."

Not knowing what to say, she chose to say nothing instead. He flopped back onto the pillow and closed his eyes. "You don't really want to be here with me, do you?"

His words took on an accusatory tone, and it stung. She recoiled, blinking. It seemed to her that he was trying to get rid of her, but was too chickenshit to tell her to leave. Instead he'd probably decided his best course of action was to get her mad enough that she left on her own.

I have to tell you, buddy, it's working like a charm. The more he said, the less she wanted to be around him. At the moment, she was barely able to resist the urge to grab her clothes and run out of his house. Out of his life. No man was worth this kind of trouble. Not even Jake. "What are you asking?"

"I know what you've been doing. You don't want to be with me. You're just trying to hurt me."

"No." It might have started out that way, but somewhere along the way she'd changed her mind. Her plan had been forgotten long ago, but fate still wouldn't let her be happy. Zack had thrown a big wrench into her life, but it shouldn't have been so huge that she and Jake couldn't have worked around it. "It's not like that. I promise. I want to be with you."

He shifted on the mattress. His chest rose and fell with each deep breath. "What about Zack?"

"Didn't we cover that earlier?"

"Not to my satisfaction. It's pretty convenient that he shows up here, out of the blue, just as we're starting to get close. Did you call him after the morning you walked out on me, or had the two of you been planning this all along?"

How dare he accuse her of something like that? True, she hadn't been honest with him from the beginning, but she'd explained her reasons and had thought he understood. How many times did she need to explain it to him? Zack was a part of her past she was ready to move beyond. Jake was the only man in her life now, but for some reason, he seemed intent on trying to push her away.

"Jake, stop it. You're acting like an ass. I don't have to sit here and put up with it."

"So don't. No one's asking you to stay."

She stilled, chewing on her lower lip while she tried to process his words. He really didn't want her around. He was doing it to her again, hurting her all over. She wouldn't have thought it possible, but this time hurt worse than the first. "Are you going to cut the crap and talk to me like a rational adult?"

"No. I'm not in the mood right now. We've been skirting around this issue for weeks, and I think it's well past time someone has the guts to drag it out into the open. I'm not stupid. Tell me the truth. For once, just give me that. You've been trying to get revenge. That's the only reason you've been with me."

She swallowed hard. How long had he known? Jake was smart. Observant. He'd probably seen it right from the beginning. "That's not the only reason. It might have been…at first…but now there's so much more there."

"So you admit that you were trying to hurt me?"

"A little, at first. But now things have changed."

"Changed, huh?" He shook his head. "You've changed. You aren't the same sweet girl I remember. You aren't even close. Now you're like every other woman out there. Telling me one thing when you really mean something else. Keeping secrets and manipulating me instead of just being honest. I can't deal with that. I have enough crap in my life without getting it from someone else, too."

Her eyes narrowed and her hands balled into fists. How dare he accuse her of changing, after what he'd done to her? She pursed her lips and stood, searching around on the floor for her clothes. Once she found them, she dressed quickly, suddenly feeling way too exposed. The urge to get out of his house—out of his life—was stronger than ever. It threatened to overpower her. Her legs shook and she could barely stand.

"You're a jerk sometimes. Do you know that? You're not the same person you were back then, either. Back then, you were a coward. And you know what? Maybe you still are. You're afraid to let yourself care about anyone. Afraid to let anyone care about you. You need to get over it, or you're never going to be truly happy."

He let out a harsh laugh. "I was pretty damned happy until you walked back into my life and started twisting me up in knots. Now everything is a fucking mess and I don't know which end is up. You wanted to hurt me? Good. Mission accomplished. You've made your point. I think it's best if we end this here and now, before it goes any further. It's been fun, but we both knew from the start that it would eventually have to come to an end."

He didn't even bother to open his eyes.

Something in her heart snapped and tears clouded her vision. She'd had her revenge, but it wasn't sweet. It left a bitter taste in her mouth and made her want to gag. His harsh words and coldness were a defense mechanism. She'd seen it before, a few times over the years, but hadn't recognized it this time until just now. She really had hurt him, and though that was what she'd wanted, it made her gut clench tight. Over the past few weeks, she'd come to realize she'd do anything to keep from hurting him, but it had already been too late.

She should have known. Should have seen that what she was doing was stupid and would only get her hurt. But she'd plowed ahead with the disaster waiting to happen anyway, and now everything had exploded in her face. Jake wouldn't forgive her for this. She didn't blame him. All her life she'd been taught that two wrongs didn't make a right, but she'd been too wrapped up in her own plans for revenge to see what she'd been doing to him. To them. She'd lost her last chance with him. He wasn't the type of man who could forgive and forget.

She walked over to his side of the bed and put her hand on his stomach. He didn't even react. Tears streamed down her cheeks and she didn't bother to swipe them away. A few of them landed on his stomach, splashing across his skin.

"Jake, please talk to me."

"No. I don't think we should talk anymore. We're done here, Amber. You assured that from the very beginning. I hope you don't get upset if I don't walk you to the door. As *drunk* as I am, I might not make it back to bed in one piece. I wouldn't want to have to be obligated to you for anything else."

She sniffled and wiped the back of her hand across her eyes. *Stupid sap, crying over him. You never wanted him in the first place.*

She hadn't, at first, but things had changed. Now she'd screwed them up and lost the only man she'd ever really wanted.

She rushed out of the room, stopping to grab her purse and keys off the table by the door before racing out of the house and down the front steps.

Once she'd driven a few blocks away, she pulled the car over and leaned on the wheel. There was no stopping the tears now, and she had a sinking suspicion there might never be.

Chapter Twelve

"What's the matter with you? You aren't acting like yourself."

Amber glanced at Zack across the table and shook her head. "Sorry. I guess I'm really not myself tonight."

She hadn't been for the past few days, since Jake had kicked her out of his house. She'd even put the opening of her business on hold, knowing she couldn't face happy couples in the state she was in. Work could wait a little longer. She had enough savings to get her through another few weeks, if need be. She figured it would take at least that long before she stopped crying every time someone mentioned his name.

She still didn't understand why she'd agreed to meet Zack for breakfast, when the last thing she wanted was to go out anywhere, with anyone. She pushed her food around on her plate, but had hardly eaten anything. Her appetite had all but disappeared.

"You miss him, don't you?" Zack asked, catching her by surprise.

"Yeah. I do." Did he expect anything less? She'd fallen hard for Jake, and to have him cut her off so completely, without any warning, had devastated her. The first day she'd been a total wreck, but had slowly started pulling herself back together. Having this conversation with Zack might cause a setback, and she dreaded having to deal with that sharp, fresh pain again.

"I'm sorry things turned out the way they did." He paused, his gaze searching, before he lifted his coffee cup to his lips and took a sip. "I never should have come here. I can't help but think some of this is my fault. All I want is for you to be happy. I can't stand to see you miserable, Amber. You mean too much to me."

"If you don't want to see me miserable, then don't look at me. At the moment, what you see is pretty much what you get." She *would* get over Jake, but it would take some time. A lot of time. She'd had her pity party the day after he'd said goodbye, and now she wanted to wallow in misery for a little while before she made the attempt to pick herself up, brush herself off, and move on with her life without him.

Her comment got a small laugh out of him. He reached out and took her hand, giving it a reassuring squeeze. "Seriously, sweetie. Is he really worth all this?"

"Probably not." But she wanted him, anyway. Her whole body ached. She should have come clean with him right from the start, before they'd gotten so involved. At least then if he'd told her he never wanted to see her again, she could have walked away unscathed. Instead she'd waited until it had been too late. Had she really expected him to forgive her, to say that what she'd done didn't matter to him?

If she had, she'd been a fool. Nobody liked to be lied to.

"Then why are you beating yourself up over this?"

"Because I was happy with him." The answer was the truth in its simplest form. Jake had made her happy. She'd felt whole when she was with him. Now she only felt ripped apart.

"And you weren't happy with me."

It was a statement, not a question, but Amber felt the need to answer, anyway. "I was happy with you, but I don't love you like you deserve. I don't think you love me, either."

Zack pulled his hand away and straightened, an agitated look on his face. He narrowed his eyes. "Of course I do. You know I love you. I've never been remiss in telling you that."

"I know you do, but not like a husband would love his wife. We've always been close, but not close enough. The connection just isn't there." She picked up a triangle of wheat toast and bit off a corner, chewing slowly. It tasted like sandpaper in her mouth.

"What you're looking for is a fairy tale. You're not going to find it, honey, because the kind of love you're looking for doesn't exist."

She said nothing, but in her heart, she knew he was wrong. That kind of love *did* exist. She'd seen it many times when engaged couples looked at each other, and it always warmed her heart. She saw it in her father's eyes when he looked at her mother, even after nearly forty years of marriage, and in Adele's eyes when she looked at Max.

It was what she felt inside every time she looked at Jake.

"I care about you," Zack continued. "A lot. That's really all that counts, isn't it? We could make it work. Come home with me, Amber. Marry me. You know we're good together."

A few weeks ago, she might have agreed, but now she couldn't. No matter how miserable she was on her own, she wouldn't settle for someone she didn't love with all her heart.

"I'm sorry, but I can't. You have to know, deep down inside, that there's someone out there who would be better for you than I could ever be."

"No. I don't know that at all. The only woman I want is you."

"Does your family have anything to do with this decision?"

His silence was answer enough. She sighed. She should have known.

"Don't do this to yourself, Zack. Be happy. You deserve it. Don't ask me to marry you because your parents tell you it's the right thing to do. Find the woman out there who completes you, the one who you can't stop thinking about even when she's right next to you, and don't settle for anyone until you find her."

Zack put his knife and fork on his plate and pushed it away. He propped his arms on the table and leaned toward her. For a second, she worried he might argue yet again, but instead he just shook his head. "How can you be so sure about all this? How do you know there's even someone like that out there?"

"Because I've seen it hundreds of times in my work. Because I've felt it in my own life. I've found the man I need."

"Think he'll take you back?"

She shook her head. *Never.* She'd ruined things with Jake, for good this time, but that didn't change the fact that she knew the right man for her was out there—just as the right woman was out there for Zack, waiting for him to find her. "I know he won't. He's stubborn and pig-headed. But I'm not going to settle—and make you miserable in the process—because of him. I'm going to move on with my life instead. Maybe I'll find someone else, and maybe I won't. Whatever happens, at least I'll know I didn't hurt you in the process."

She'd hurt one important man in her life, and she refused to be selfish enough to hurt another.

"Is there anything I can do to help?"

"Just let yourself be happy for you, instead of living life for your family. That would make me very happy."

She stood and smoothed her sundress down her legs. "I'm sorry, but I have to go. My mother's birthday party starts in an hour and I still have to find her a gift. Will I see you later?"

"I'm going back home tonight. Vacation's over, you know, time to get back to work before my father sends out a search party. But I'll call you soon."

"Promise?"

"Of course. Have I ever let you down?"

"No. You haven't."

Zack deserved someone who would be good to him instead of a woman who spent all her time thinking of someone else. He'd find the right woman, too. Amber knew it in her heart.

ભ ભ ભ

Jake stopped and took a fortifying breath before he dared to open the gate and walk into the Velezes' backyard. Music and laughter from Regina's party floated through the air and he swallowed hard. This was one party he hadn't even wanted to come to, but instead had been coerced into under extreme duress. His mother had quite a memory for things he'd done growing up. She remembered things he himself had forgotten all about, and there were things he didn't want made public. Like his grade school photos, or the fact that he'd been suspended in fifth grade for putting a frog in his teacher's lunch bag.

He hadn't wanted to skip the party because of Regina. He just hadn't wanted to run into Amber and Zack. Last time he'd seen her, he'd made a complete ass out of himself. He deserved it if she never spoke to him again, but he couldn't stand to sit back and watch her act all lovey-dovey with the rich guy from New York.

"What are you waiting for?" David's voice came from behind him. "A written invitation?"

"Not hardly. I have a feeling there might be one or two people who don't want me here at all."

David walked up beside him and smiled. "You're talking about Amber, right? What happened between the two of you, anyway?"

"I had a few drinks and acted like a supreme asshole. I chased her away, and it'll be a friggin' miracle if she talks to me again."

"Why am I not surprised?"

"Probably because I'm a moron." Jake shook his head. "I can't do this. I'm going home. Tell Regina I said happy birthday, okay?"

He started to walk away, but David grabbed his arm. "No way are you getting out of this. Get your ass in there and make happy."

"I'm not in the mood."

"Too bad." David wouldn't take no for an answer. He gave Jake a nudge toward the gate, opened it, and pushed him inside.

Once inside, Regina spotted them and Jake had no choice but to stay. He resigned himself to pretending he was happy—until he spotted Amber across the crowded yard.

Even in such a big group, she stood out. She wore a bright blue sundress and a huge smile as she stood to the side of the yard, near the fence, deep in conversation with Madison. Steve was right behind his wife, his hand on her waist. That fact brought a smile to Jake's face. Steve had called a few nights earlier and told Jake he and Madison had decided to forget about the divorce. Things looked to be on the mend for the two of them, and as much as he hated to admit it, Amber had been instrumental in their reunion.

Amber's gaze came up to Jake's and she stopped talking for a second. All too soon, she broke the connection and pretended like she hadn't seen him at all.

His stomach bottomed out. *Damn it.* She couldn't even look at him. This promised to be one hell of a long day.

ൠ ൠ ൠ

Amber didn't know how she did it, but somehow she managed to make it to the halfway point in her mother's party without screaming or crying or running away. Seeing Jake had been a shock, even though she'd expected him to be there. To his credit, he hadn't glared at her or made any scathing remarks.

A few minutes later, Madison walked over to her. "Your mother asked me to have you get another package of paper plates out of the storage room in the basement. She said she was running low."

Amber glanced at the food table and the giant stack of paper plates on top and shook her head. "You have to be kidding me."

"Nope." Madison smiled. "She said she just wants to be prepared. She's afraid she might run out and wouldn't want people to have to wait for someone to get more if that happened."

"Typical. Okay, if it makes her feel better, I guess I'll be back in a few minutes."

Once in the basement storage room, she grabbed the step ladder from the corner and stood on it to reach the packages of plates her mother kept on the top shelf. Leave it to her mother, the original queen of the organized, to worry about running out of plates when she had a stack of at least a hundred already out there.

Footsteps sounded from the doorway, and a second later, she heard Jake's voice. "Oh, sorry. I didn't know you were in here. If I had, I would have waited."

"It's fine. Come in. Get whatever you need. I'm done in here, anyway."

He'd no sooner stepped into the room then the door shut behind him. The click of the lock followed.

Chapter Thirteen

What the hell? Jake rushed to the door and tried the knob, but it wouldn't budge. "It's stuck."

"No," Amber told him, her tone defeated. "It's locked. I heard it click."

"Locked? You've got to be kidding me." He pounded the door with his fists. "Hey! Is anybody out there? Unlock the door so we can get out."

"No point in yelling. Do you really think this is an accident?"

He closed his eyes and let his forehead drop to the door. Of all the sick jokes. As if he needed this right now, on top of the mess his life had become. "I'm sorry. If I'd known they were going to do this, I wouldn't have come down here."

"It's not your fault." She said the words, but her tone told him she didn't believe them.

He closed his eyes and pictured her in his mind. He could see her standing behind him, arms crossed over her chest, her lips pursed and her eyes narrowed. He could also picture the shape of her body under the little sundress she wore, and that image was what made him curse. Her scent filled the closet, torturing his mind and his body. He wanted her even now, even after all that had happened between them.

She had a right to her anger. He hadn't been nice. But he had a right to his, too. She'd screwed him over. She'd said she cared, but that had been a lie. And now he was stuck in here with her for who the hell knew how long.

What a fucking mess.

"Jake?" Amber's voice was surprisingly soft and it hit him low in the gut.

He pressed his palms to the door. "What?"

"Why did you walk away from me all those years ago?"

Shit. Not the time or place he wanted to rehash his cowardice. He wasn't done being mad at her yet. "I already explained it to you. I was young. Stupid. And…"

No way. He couldn't tell her the truth. Not all of it. Not if he wanted to walk away from her with his sanity intact.

She had Zack. The perfect, rich fiancé who could give her everything she wanted. She'd be a fool not to go back to the guy. A guy who obviously loved her so much.

But not as much as Jake did. No one could ever love her that much. He'd spent practically his whole life wanting her.

"And what?" Her warm palm landed on his back and he flinched. He hadn't even heard her approach.

"And nothing. It is what it is. I can't explain it."

"Will you try? For me?"

She rested her cheek on his back. His throat closed up and he moved closer to the door, hoping it would suck him in and get him out of this room. A room that had suddenly become way too small. She asked too much of him. He'd never said the words to a woman he wasn't related to. Never. Had never even planned on saying them. But if Amber wanted to hear them, he was powerless to stop himself.

"I loved you. That scared me. I didn't want to be in love."

Her hands came around his waist and splayed across his stomach. The muscles under her touch contracted.

"Why didn't you tell me? We could have worked it out together."

"That's the thing. I didn't know if I wanted to be together. I did, but at the same time, I didn't. We were going away to separate colleges, and I was looking at law school, too. I just wanted to...I don't know."

"You just wanted to be a college kid. To have fun and not have to worry about obligations and long-distance relationships."

"Yeah. I didn't want to be tied down to an engagement at eighteen."

"We wouldn't have rushed things."

"That's the kicker. I wanted to rush them. That was what scared me most of all. Now I fucked things up for good. I never should have touched you. Never should have walked away, either."

"I'm glad you did."

He stiffened. She couldn't be serious. After everything that had happened since she'd come back to town, she was going to start with this? "Why?"

"I like who I am now. I'm not shy, and I'm not afraid. I never would have had the guts to change my life if you hadn't walked out. I would have been stuck in a rut. When I moved back here, I wasn't over what had happened. At least not entirely. I am now, though."

"Really?" An emotion he refused to name clogged his throat. "Don't just say that."

"I'm not. I mean it." She sighed. "Jake, I loved you then, too. I think I always had, and no matter how much I tried to convince myself otherwise, I don't think I ever really stopped."

He shrugged out of her touch and moved to the back of the closet, trying to put as much space between them as he could. The air was suddenly so thick with her scent he couldn't draw a full breath.

He didn't need her confessions. Not now. Not when she had another man waiting for her. She'd either leave with Zack, or convince him to stay here. Either way, Jake couldn't take it.

Her frustrated sigh echoed across the pantry. "Why do you keep pushing me away?"

"It's not just me. We've been doing it to each other. Maybe even from the start." He shook his head. Could this be any harder? If so, he didn't see how. "We should just sit and wait for someone to think we've been alone long enough. Eventually someone has to unlock that door. They wouldn't leave us in here to run out of air or starve."

"Jake, please. Can't we just talk without fighting or ignoring each other?"

No. He already knew the answer to that. There was no way he could sit back and think about her leaving with another man and not get upset about it.

He slammed his hand against the cement wall, but wished he could take the action back when Amber flinched. "What's the point in hashing this out to no end? It's just going to make us both hurt, and it's not going to solve anything."

"Why do you say that?"

"You have Zack, who has to be the most fucking perfect man on the face of the planet. What do you need me for? I just end up pissing you off eventually. Every friggin' time."

"Zack went back to New York."

Jake stared at her for a few minutes, trying to process the information. He wouldn't get his hopes up. Not yet. "When are you following him?"

"Um, like, *never*."

The sexy smile she gave him had not only his hopes up, but other parts of his body, too. He leaned back against the wall and let out a breath. "You're staying here? Why the hell would you want to do that?"

"Because you're here."

"What does that have to do with anything?"

"Did you miss that whole sappy love declaration thing a few minutes ago?"

"No. I didn't believe it. I thought you were trying to make me feel better."

"You should know by now that I would never do anything just to spare your feelings." She walked closer, her hips swaying with every step, until she stood only inches from him. He squirmed under the intense scrutiny in her gaze. "What I feel for you is real, and it's not going away."

"I never wanted to get married."

"I know that. I never asked that of you. I like you just the way you are, flaws and all."

He opened his mouth to speak, but she wrapped her hand around his neck and dragged him down for a kiss. She trailed her free hand down his stomach until she reached his fly, and then she kept going. All rational thought fled his mind as the blood left his head and made its way to a point further south. A point that now stood at full attention.

Soon her fingers were on the button at the top of his jeans and she'd worked it free. His zipper rasped as she pulled it down, but he grabbed her wrists before she could go any further.

"Slow down. This is happening way too fast."

She only laughed. "Isn't that supposed to be the woman's line?"

"I just want to get a few things straight first. You're not leaving?"

She shook her head.

"You're not getting back together with Zack?"

"I told you he left. How much more clear can I make this? I want you, Jake, and if you still want me, I think we have a perfect opportunity for a little alone time here. Let's not waste it trying to sort through things we can work out later." She stepped back, took her panties off, and dropped them to the floor. "Do you want to talk, or is there something else you'd rather be doing?"

"Talk? Who said anything about talking?" Like he could even think straight right now. He walked toward her, crushed her body against his, and kissed her.

Instantly, a thousand sensations battered him. It had been way too long since he'd held her. Touched her and kissed her. Days. He wouldn't let it go that long again—because from this moment on, he was never letting her out of his sight for more than a few hours.

Over the past few days, he'd come to a harsh realization. He needed her. Couldn't think about living without her.

And he'd done all he could to make sure she never spoke to him again.

He was damned lucky she'd forgiven him. After the things he'd said, he didn't deserve her forgiveness, but he'd take it. At this point, he'd take whatever he could get from her.

She reached between them and slipped her hand inside his boxers, cradling his cock in her palm. Her warm hand stroked up and down the length until she'd driven him nearly mad with want for her.

When he couldn't take it anymore, he broke the kiss, backed her against the wall, and hiked her legs up around his hips. He thrust into her and groaned from the amazing feel of her hot, wet sex enveloping him. *Shit.*

He rested his forehead against hers. "We can't do this."

She arched her hips, pulling him even deeper. "Why not? You were doing fine a second ago."

"I…uh, don't have anything with me."

"I'm on the pill. Have been for a long time. We're okay."

"Are you sure about this?"

She nodded. "But we should hurry. We probably don't have long before the jerk who locked us in here has a change of heart and comes back to let us out."

That was all he needed to hear. He thrust into her over and over, reveling in the feel of her wet heat surrounding him. She clutched at his shoulders and dropped her head back against the wall, her legs tightening even more around his waist. And then, amazingly, she came. Her lips parted, and though she didn't cry out, a smile crept up the corners of her mouth.

The feel of her inner muscles squeezing him, trying to draw him deeper, prodded him to thrust harder. Faster. Soon he was rocking into her, out of control. She leaned in and kissed the side of his neck, and that was enough to push him over the edge into his own orgasm.

He pressed his forehead to hers and closed his eyes. Since he'd chased her away, he'd been trying to think of a way to get her back, but something in the back of his mind told him it was hopeless. That she'd never speak to him again after some of the things he'd said. Now everything had changed. Maybe they'd finally be able to put the hurt behind them, once and for all, and start over again.

He stepped back, pulling out of her, and gave her a quick, soft kiss. "Are you okay?"

Amber smiled. "Never better. Not ever."

ભ ભ ભ

Jake was just getting his shirt buttoned when the click of the lock echoed through the room. Amber ran her hand down his arm. "We're free."

"Maybe I don't want to be."

"Would you rather stay here in this hot pantry all day?" She laughed, but her gaze caught his and her laughter stopped. "Jake? What is it?"

"I want to be with you."

"Yeah, I think we just established that pretty well a few minutes ago. If you want, we could go back to my place and establish it again if you think that would help."

He couldn't help but laugh, but soon all his humor faded away. "No. That's not what I want."

"I thought you did."

"I do, but that's not what I'm talking about here." He finished buttoning his shirt, tucked it into his jeans and zipped them up. "Not to be crass or anything, I want a lot more than an occasional screw in a closet."

She straightened her dress and started backing toward the door. "I think we need to get out of here. The lack of air has obviously addled your mind."

"My mind is fine. In fact, I don't think it's ever been better. There's something I have to say to you."

"Jake?"

He walked to her and tugged her in for a fast, hard kiss. When he broke away, he looked into her eyes. "Marry me."

He'd meant to tell her he loved her, but the proposal had slipped out instead. She made him crazy. He couldn't even think straight around her. Funny thing was, Amber as his wife was the only thing he really wanted.

"Don't joke around like that."

"I'm not joking. I've never been more serious. Marry me, Amber. You know it feels right. I love you."

She looked like she might turn him down for a second, but then a smile spread over her face. "This is nuts. We haven't even been seeing each other for a month."

"Yeah."

"You don't want to get married."

"Didn't. That's changed."

"We shouldn't."

"Yeah, we should."

She shook her head. "Okay. If you're crazy enough to ask, I'm crazy enough to say yes."

He was crazy enough to do anything she wanted. Whatever she asked for, he'd give it to her. "Good. If I have to be crazy, I'm glad I'm not the only one."

Amber's expression turned serious. "Just one thing, though."

"What's that?"

"I really don't want a big wedding."

"No problem. You can have whatever kind of wedding you want. Your choice. You're the wedding planner."

"Our mothers won't understand."

"I'll talk to them." He said the words, but he didn't know how much good they'd do. Separately, Miriam Storm and Regina Velez were forces to be reckoned with. Teamed together, and Jake doubted it was even worth the fight. Come November, he had a feeling they'd be walking down the aisle, Amber dressed in that white gown she said she didn't want. Oddly enough, he found himself actually looking forward to it.

೮೪ ೮೪ ೮೪

Steve walked over to Jake and handed him a beer.

"Thanks." Jake took the bottle and brought it to his lips for a big gulp. When he lowered the bottle, he sighed. Finally, something to wet his parched throat. "I really need this."

"Yeah." Steve laughed. "It must have been hot down there in that closet. And with the two of you down there alone, I'm sure that made it even hotter."

"Excuse me?"

"You know. The door locked, hardly any ventilation. Not to mention the fact that you and Amber probably steamed things up a little."

"How did you know that?"

"Anyone standing outside the door would have known. Between the two of us, you and Amber really aren't that quiet."

Jake glared at his friend. What the hell had Steve done? "Did you lock us in there?"

"It was Madison's idea. At least that's what she tells me, but I think your mother may have planted the seed in her head."

It should surprise him, but it didn't. Leave it to his mother to have the final say in everyone's life decisions. "Why?"

"You and Amber did a good thing for me and Maddie. I had to repay you somehow. The way we saw it, the two of you needed to see you were acting like idiots. Mission accomplished, huh?"

Jake stared at where Amber stood across the lawn, flanked by Madison and Adele. The three women were laughing at something. Amber looked his way and smiled, and his heart hitched. "You could say that. I'm getting married."

Steve, who'd been taking a sip of his beer, sputtered and coughed. It took him a few seconds to recover. "Excuse me? Could you repeat that? I think I must have heard you wrong."

"I don't think you did. I asked Amber to marry me. She said yes."

"Tell me you're not serious."

"I'm very serious." More serious than he'd been about anything in his life.

"Well, congrats, I guess. Another one bites the dust."

Jake laughed. "Amber is special to me. She always has been. I was a moron before, and I'm lucky she forgave me. She could just as easily have spit in my face."

"She's not totally innocent here."

"Yeah. I kind of like that about her." Jake glanced at Steve and shook his head. "No one has ever interested me the way she does. That has to say something."

"If she can put a ball and chain on your ankle, of all people, that's saying a lot. She must be an amazing woman."

"She is. And I'm the luckiest man on the planet."

"I'd have to argue with you there."

"Go ahead. I know I'm right." Jake slapped Steve on the shoulder. "This is all your fault, you know."

"Is that a thank you?"

"You know it is. I owe you one."

"No. You got me and Maddie back together. I'd say we're pretty much even."

Jake knew that wasn't true. He had to be the damned luckiest man on the planet. Madison was a great woman, but she wasn't Amber. No other woman would ever do it for him again. It had taken him way too long to realize what she meant to him, but now that he had her right where he wanted her, he didn't ever plan to let her go.

About the Author

Born in Gloucester, Massachusetts, Elisa Adams has lived most of her life on the east coast. Formerly a nursing assistant and phlebotomist, writing has been a longtime hobby. Now a full time writer, she lives on the New Hampshire border with her three children.

To learn more about Elisa, please visit http://www.elisaadams.com/. Send an email to Elisa Adams at elisa@elisaadams.com or join her Yahoo! Monthly Newsletter group to keep up to date with Elisa and her projects http://groups.yahoo.com/group/ElisaAdams/

Samhain Publishing, Ltd.

It's all about the story...

Action/Adventure
Fantasy
Historical
Horror
Mainstream
Mystery/Suspense
Non-Fiction
Paranormal
Red Hots!
Romance
Science Fiction
Western
Young Adult

http://www.samhainpublishing.com